NOWHERE TO RUN, NOWHERE TO HIDE

The quiet was unnerving. He expected to hear probing shots from the two men, but their rifles were silent. He scrambled to higher ground, traversed the most dangerous stretch, and started looking for the rocks that marked the hiding place of the bushwhackers.

Lew dropped to his belly when he caught sight of the spot where the two men had lain in ambush. He was quiet, but one or both of them must have seen him, because the stillness exploded with the crackling sound of two rifle shots very close together. The brush above Lew rattled as bullets tore through the leaves. He heard the brittle sound of branches breaking. The two rifles fired again and bullets plowed gouges in the earth just below him. Dirt spattered his face and he rolled downhill a few feet and took up a position behind a small boulder. Bullets spanged against it and he knew the two men had him cold . . .

THE VIGILANTE

SANTA FE SHOWDOWN

Jory Sherman

BERKLEY BOOKS, NEW YORK

THE BERKLEY PUBLISHING GROUP
Published by the Penguin Group
Penguin Group (USA) Inc.
375 Hudson Street, New York, New York 10014, USA
Penguin Group (Canada), 90 Eglinton Avenue East, Suite 700, Toronto, Ontario M4P 2Y3, Canada
(a division of Pearson Penguin Canada Inc.)
Penguin Books Ltd., 80 Strand, London WC2R 0RL, England
Penguin Group Ireland, 25 St. Stephen's Green, Dublin 2, Ireland (a division of Penguin Books Ltd.)
Penguin Group (Australia), 250 Camberwell Road, Camberwell, Victoria 3124, Australia
(a division of Pearson Australia Group Pty. Ltd.)
Penguin Books India Pvt. Ltd., 11 Community Centre, Panchsheel Park, New Delhi—110 017, India
Penguin Group (NZ), 67 Apollo Drive, Rosedale, North Shore 0632, New Zealand
(a division of Pearson New Zealand Ltd.)
Penguin Books (South Africa) (Pty.) Ltd., 24 Sturdee Avenue, Rosebank, Johannesburg 2196,
South Africa

Penguin Books Ltd., Registered Offices: 80 Strand, London WC2R 0RL, England

This is a work of fiction. Names, characters, places, and incidents either are the product of the author's imagination or are used fictitiously, and any resemblance to actual persons, living or dead, business establishments, events, or locales is entirely coincidental.

THE VIGILANTE: SANTA FE SHOWDOWN

A Berkley Book / published by arrangement with the author

PRINTING HISTORY
Berkley edition / December 2007

Copyright © 2007 by Jory Sherman.
Cover illustration by Bruce Emmett.
Cover design by Steven Ferlauto.

ISBN: 978-0-425-21445-9

BERKLEY®
Berkley Books are published by The Berkley Publishing Group,
a division of Penguin Group (USA) Inc.,
375 Hudson Street, New York, New York 10014.
BERKLEY is a registered trademark of Penguin Group (USA) Inc.
The "B" design is a trademark belonging to Penguin Group (USA) Inc.

PRINTED IN THE UNITED STATES OF AMERICA

10 9 8 7 6 5 4 3 2 1

For Midge Rosenbaum

1

LEW ZANE STARED STRAIGHT INTO THE EYES OF MARSHAL
Horatio Blackhawk. Dark black eyes like velvet flint. It was
like staring into a pair of gun barrels. He saw the shiny
badge on the man's vest, the way he slouched against the
building with his tall, lanky frame, his right hand free and
lazing next to his low-slung holster.

Blackhawk looked at Zane, then touched a finger to the
brim of his hat.

Zane returned the salute.

Blackhawk smiled.

And waited.

"You could arrest me now, take me back to Arkansas,"
Lew said. "I'm a wanted man."

"You are. And I could."

"Are you going to?"

"I'm thinking about it real hard, Zane."

"If you give a damn about justice, you won't. What's your
name, anyway? Judge Wyman send you?"

"The name's Blackhawk. Horatio Blackhawk. No, I work
out of Springfield, up in Missouri. But Wyman called for
your arrest. I got the case."

"You ever meet Wyman?"

"I met him. Look, Zane, I went over your case pretty thorough-like. I think you got caught up in a gauntlet down there in Carroll County. The people who want you, got blood in their eyes, for sure. But I'm bound to uphold the law."

"The law? What law is that?"

"United States law, son."

"If it isn't any different from Arkansas law, it's pretty piss poor."

"I'm not going to argue the law with you, Zane. I got a warrant for your arrest."

"And that makes everything right, according to you. You're bound to serve it."

"Yes."

"And take me back to Berryville in irons."

"If necessary."

Somewhere up the street, a dog barked. A tinker's cart rolled past, its innards ringing with faint chimes. A mountain jay squawked at the vendor's horse, dove down close to the animal's ears, then flapped away to land on a watering trough where it regarded its reflection with a cocked head, then began to preen its feathers with a pointed black stylus of a beak.

"Do you know why the judge wants me back in his court, Marshal?"

"That's the judge's business. I only serve warrants, carry out the court's wishes. Look, Zane, I talked to everybody down there, in Osage, Alpena, Green Forest, Berryville. You got two scared women after your hide, Abigail Pope and Sarah Canby. They want to see your neck stretched."

"Why would those women be afraid of me?" Lew asked.

"They think you might come back and kill them, like you killed their sons and husbands, I reckon."

"I wouldn't do that."

"I don't think you would, but . . ."

"Wiley Pope and Fritz Canby murdered my folks. In cold blood. They tried to kill me. I don't hold their mothers to blame for what they did."

"Their fathers tried to kill you, too, didn't they?"

"Yeah. They kidnapped Seneca Jones to draw me out,

so's they could put my lights out. Sheriff Colfax was in on it, too."

"Those women have a reason to fear you, I gathered, when I asked around Alpena. They hold a big grudge."

"I don't. Carrying a grudge is like toting two hundred pounds of lead on your back."

"Good way to look at it, I reckon." Blackhawk felt in his shirt pocket and pulled out a pack of cigarettes. He shook one out, put it to his lips, and held out the pack to Lew. Lew shook his head. Blackhawk put the pack back in his pocket, withdrew a match. He cocked a boot up and struck the match on the side of the heel. He touched the flame to his cigarette and drew the smoke into his lungs. He let it out slow, as if he had all the time in the world to stand there and chew the fat with a wanted man, a man with a price on his head.

"You aim to collect the bounty on me?" Lew said.

"Not eligible. I'm just doing my job."

"Do you like what you do?"

"Most of the time, yes. I don't like criminals much."

Lew said nothing as Blackhawk stood there and smoked as if there were nothing urgent on his mind.

Memories of his parents bubbled up to the surface in Lew's mind. He thought of that day in the woods when he had seen them for the last time and then stepped out the door. He had hiked up the road, killed the deer, dressed it out, then gotten the news that his mother and father had been murdered. On his birthday. The sadness of that day welled up in him. He had never wanted revenge for their murders. Two young men his own age, men he knew, had killed them. All he had wanted was justice. But he was thwarted on every side by the Alpena sheriff, the judge in Berryville, almost everyone. Finally, he had gone after Wiley and Fritz himself. The Alpena sheriff had come after him and tried to kill him. He had shot all three men in self-defense. But now there was a bounty on his head, and a warrant for his arrest. He was wanted for murder, although anyone with any brains would know he was innocent.

"I guess what it boils down to," Blackhawk said, "is that you can't go around being a vigilante. That's what they're calling you back home in Arkansas."

"I'm not a vigilante. I just want justice."

"You know what the Mexes say about that."

"No," Lew said.

"No hay justicia en el mundo."

Lew know what it meant. He had picked up some Spanish since coming to Colorado.

"There is no justice in the world," Lew said. "The Mexicans are pretty smart, I'd say."

"I think they meant there was no justice for them," Blackhawk said.

"And none for me."

Blackhawk finished his cigarette and ground it out under his boot heel.

"Maybe you'll get a fair trial. Get a good lawyer—that's my advice."

"My lawyer helped me get away from that mess back home."

"You ever plan to go back one day?"

"No. There's nothing there for me anymore."

"What about your gal? Seneca Jones."

Lew felt a rush of hot blood to his face. He hadn't thought of Seneca in days. He could hardly remember her face anymore.

"She's not my gal."

"Oh? She pines for you. I could tell that when I talked to her."

"You spoke to Seneca?"

"I talked to everybody, near 'bouts, in Osage. But that Seneca, she's a-waitin' for you, sure enough."

"I miss her sometimes. She was a good friend."

Blackhawk gave out a short laugh.

"More than a friend, according to her."

Lew felt the redness on his face, like a stain. He touched a hand to his cheek. His skin was hot. But he knew he couldn't go back there. They'd put him in jail and throw away the key.

He shook his head.

"I'm not going back to Osage."

"Never? What if you get acquitted at trial?"

"I don't aim to go to trial, Marshal."

Blackhawk's attitude changed. His face hardened and a muscle quivered along his jawline.

"These papers I got says different."

"I'm not guilty of anything, Marshal."

"These papers . . ."

"I know, they say I'm a murderer. The murderers are in the ground, where they belong. That court should have hanged them, but it didn't."

"Like I said, Zane. You get a good lawyer, and you stand a good chance of going free."

"If you take me back, Mr. Blackhawk, I doubt I'll ever get a trial."

"What makes you say that?"

"I know those people back home. They already showed me their colors. They'll fix me up in a jailbreak or something and I'll get a bullet in the back. No one will lift a finger. That's how it works back home. That's why I'm not going back. I didn't want revenge when I went after those boys; I wanted justice. And every time I tried to get some, somebody shoved a gun barrel in my face."

"You sound pretty bitter, Zane."

"No, I'm not bitter. What's done is done. I got another life now and I try to stay out of trouble."

"You got in a heap of trouble up on the mountain. You don't look like somebody who runs from trouble. Not to me, you don't."

"Carol Smith wanted justice, too. I helped her get some, maybe."

"The vigilante again."

"Look, Blackhawk, if you were not a lawman and you were in a town where there was no law, what would you do?"

"I don't know. I reckon I'd send for the law."

"What if there was no law to come? What if you were a decent man and the town was full of lawbreakers? What if you saw injustice at every corner? Would you just stand by and let the criminals take over the town?"

"No, I don't reckon I would."

"When there is no law, you have to be the law."

"That what you say about all this back in Alpena?"

"The law turned the other way. My folks were plumb murdered. I went to the law and the sheriff up there told me to bury my folks and go on about my business."

"That doesn't give you the right . . ."

"Yes it does. When there is no law, Blackhawk, and something's not right, you have to become the law. That's what I did. Plain and simple."

"You became a vigilante. Judge, jury, and executioner."

"It might look that way, unless you were in it. Like a whirlwind out on the plains. Kind of pretty to watch, and funny, sometimes—but if you're in the middle of it, getting whipped to death by wind, rocks, sticks, and sand, it's pure hell."

"Did you kill Jeff Stevens?" Blackhawk asked, point blank.

"What?"

"Somebody says you killed Stevens and robbed him."

"That somebody is a liar."

"I didn't think it was true. But you got more problems than just me, Zane."

"I wouldn't be surprised. Trouble seems to follow me."

"Bolivar has caught up with you, in case you didn't know."

"Bolivar?"

"You know, where Carol is from. She and her father, Jeff Stevens. Both from Bolivar."

"I know that."

"Carol's a married woman. And like you, she's got a price on her head."

"I don't get you, Marshal."

"Her husband, Wayne Smith, took out a big insurance policy on the lady and their kids."

"And?"

"I think he wants to hang you and get rid of his wife and kids, live off the insurance money."

"How do you know all this?" Lew asked.

"I talked to Wayne Smith yesterday."

"He's here in Pueblo?"

"Looking for you, Zane."

"I heard he was a criminal himself. Stole some money back in Bolivar."

"True. I think he's got his sights set on Santa Fe. What he told me, anyway."

"Why don't you arrest him?"

"I'm considering it."

"Looks like you've got a full plate, Mr. Blackhawk."

Just then, both men stiffened as they heard a woman scream from inside the Fountain Hotel. Then they heard a gunshot, followed by two more. A man inside the hotel yelled something.

"Carol," Lew said.

Blackhawk drew his pistol and dashed inside the hotel before Lew could move. He heard more noises inside.

"Stop him," a man yelled.

Lew drew his revolver and dashed through the door. He saw Blackhawk taking the stairs two steps at a time. The clerk stared at him, wild-eyed, as he ran up the stairs. There was another shot, and a man staggered toward Lew and fell at his feet, mortally wounded.

Lew heard the crash of breaking glass and thumps on the back roof. Down the hall, he saw a man scramble through a window and disappear. Blackhawk lay on the floor in front of an open door, dead or unconscious, Lew didn't know which.

Lew ran to the window and looked out in time to see a man on the roof turn and look at him. The man had a gun in his hand and he pointed it straight at Lew.

Lew ducked just as the man squeezed the trigger. But he saw the sheriff's badge on his shirt and knew, instantly, who it was. When he raised up his head again, he saw the man fly off the roof and heard him hit the ground with a thud.

Lew turned and walked back to where Blackhawk lay still in front of the open doorway.

He bent down and put a finger beneath the marshal's ear. There was a pulse. There was also a bump on the side of his head, swelling to a rosy egg. Blackhawk was out cold.

There was a silence now that issued from inside the room with the open door.

Lew stepped inside, his hands suddenly clammy.

He held his Colt at the ready, crouching to stay low.

There was blood everywhere—on the floor, the walls. The children were on the bed, sprawled there like broken dolls, their heads twisted as if they had tried to get away. They were covered with blood, and neither was breathing.

On the other side of the bed, Lew found Carol. She had her shotgun clutched in one hand, lying by her side. She hadn't had the chance to fire it.

There was a dark hole in her chest, blood all around it. A bullet hole.

Lew felt something squeeze his chest, and he struggled for air as his stomach churned, his knees turned to rubber.

He knelt down beside Carol and touched her forehead. Her eyes were closed. He pried one of them open with his forefinger and saw the frosty glaze of death. He winced and squeezed back the tears that boiled from his eyes.

The children were dead. Carol was dead.

Blackhawk was unconscious.

Wayne Smith had gotten away. Lew knew that it was Smith who had murdered his own family.

For the money.

Greed.

That's what drove Wayne Smith. Pure greed.

Lew knew he was going to be sick. He needed air and he needed to get away before he was blamed for the carnage in that hotel room.

What had Blackhawk said? Wayne Smith might be heading for Santa Fe. That was it.

New Mexico.

Well, that was where Lew had to go, then. He knew that.

He had fallen in love with Carol. They might have had a future together after she divorced her husband.

That future was gone. Wiped away by a crooked sheriff who thought only of himself.

He stepped past Blackhawk.

"Some other time, Mr. Blackhawk," Lew whispered, and walked down the hall.

Twenty minutes later, he was atop his horse, Ruben, heading west.

He had gotten a good look at Wayne Smith.

He would know him when he saw him.

"Maybe I am a vigilante, Ruben, old boy," he said. "What do you think?"

Ruben snorted and whickered softly, shaking his head. Lew studied the road ahead. There were fresh horse tracks in the dirt. He touched spurs to Ruben's flanks. Smith was lighting a shuck, for sure, putting distance between himself and the murders he had committed.

Ruben strode into a slow canter. A roadrunner, what the Mexicans called a *paisano*, streaked across the road in front of Lew. Ruben didn't swerve an inch. Ahead, blue sky and fluffy white clouds painted shadows across a desolate, empty land.

And Carol in his thoughts, and Seneca Jones, too. The girls he left behind.

2

A FEW MOMENTS LATER, LEW REALIZED HE WAS NOT FOLLOW-ing just one man, Wayne Smith, but three. Two other riders had apparently been waiting for Smith. The tracks closely paralleled each other. He saw where Smith's companions had joined him on the road. When he looked off in the direction from which the tracks had come, he saw a low flat mesa and some little hills, any one of which would have made a good place for a lookout.

The mountains were still mantled in snow, but the foothills were streaming with runoff from the spring melt, stippled with shoots of green grass. Fountain Creek was running high, its surface frothy and choked with driftwood and clumps of earth that broke up and sank or were absorbed by the water.

A wave of homesickness swept over him. Spring in the Ozarks was the time of year Lew liked best. That was when the redbuds bloomed and the dogwoods were like bright lights in the green hills. The air was filled with the fragrance of tree blossoms and the fields were losing their drab khaki color and greening out under a warm sun.

The mountains gleamed like alabaster, so purely white and blinding, they snatched the breath from his mouth. He had been in them not so long ago, and now, he realized, they were in him. He had become a western man, like so many others before him who had come to the Rocky Mountains, gazed upon them and felt their majesty, their brooding time-lessness, the weight of countless centuries. The mountains were bigger than the Ozark hills, and the sky was broader, more blue, and closer somehow. It was a good land, rich with unknown treasure, lying fallow for any who chose to stay and farm. His blood raced and tingled with the thought of settling in such country, someday, maybe, when he no longer had to outrun the posters that bore his likeness and his name.

The ground and the road were soft and moist. They held the tracks good, and they were so fresh, the moisture in them was just turning to steam under the blaze of the warming sun.

He wished he had not seen what Wayne had done to Carol. Even now, he was trying to erase that image of her dead face and replace it with the smiling woman he had known in the mountains, the woman he had fallen in love with, despite the fact that she was married and had children. Her true face swam in memory, then was replaced by Seneca's face. She had come back to him, in memory, at this hour of his grief, this sullen gray grief that threatened to blot out the sun, deafen him to the lyrical chirping of birds, blind him to the empty road ahead.

And why was he here? Was he running from Blackhawk like a rabbit? Or was he, as Blackhawk had said, a vigilante bent on vengeance against the man who had murdered the woman he loved? The marshal would have arrested him and taken him back to Arkansas, probably to be tried by a kanga-roo court and hanged before he reached his twenty-first birthday. He had to admit it. He was on the run again, run-ning from the law, the law that had not been fair with him in the past. But he was honest enough with himself to know that he was also bent on bringing Wayne Smith to justice. It galled him to think that Carol's husband would profit by her death, her murder.

He wondered if Blackhawk would have forsaken the war-rants in his pocket and gone after Wayne Smith, who had been caught in the act, practically. Probably not. The murder was a local matter, to be handled by the authorities in Pueblo. But Smith had escaped any retribution. He was headed for Santa Fe. Out of sight and out of mind of the Pueblo police, probably.

Was there justice in the world? He had once thought so. But now he was no longer sure. He was a wanted man, but all he had done was defend himself. Yes, he had gone after Wiley Pope and Fritz Canby, but only because the sheriff in Alpena would not, because he was loyal to the men who paid his salary, the men who made the town prosperous.

There was no justice in that, and certainly no fairness.

Lew was becoming bitter, despite his intentions to the contrary, and he tried to shake it off. He did not want to become a bitter man, disillusioned by life. Carol had stirred something in his heart, made him feel alive and strong, protective of her and of her children. That's who he was, or who he wanted to be, a man who was needed, who could care for a woman and make her happy, be a father to her children and his own.

The land rose under him slightly, and as he topped the rise, expecting to see only open spaces and the long road, he came upon a white woolly sea and a sound he had never heard before. There upon the plain, and blocking the road, a huge herd of bleating sheep grazed and milled, while a furry black and white dog raced up and down the nearest side, pushing back strays.

A man walked along among the sheep, a staff in his hand. Two boys with sticks chased sheep, and far to the east, a woman and a girl sat in a small covered wagon that creaked and groaned, clattering with pots and pans. The wagon was pulled by a pair of mules, their hides moth-eaten, worn smooth in places by the rub of the traces. The two boys, wading through the herd of sheep, looked like a couple of pollywogs cavorting in a foamy tide.

Lew's way was blocked for miles. He stood up in the stirrups to try to see beyond, but there was no trace of the three riders he had been following. There were sheep as far as he could see, in every direction. They had not yet crossed

Fountain Creek, but they seemed to be headed that way. He had never seen sheep before, and it was a strange sight. Their bleating filled the air, and he watched as the little black and white dog herded bunches of them back into the herd. It was fascinating to watch it work as the man walked along with his staff, seemingly as carefree as a man could be.

Lew rode toward the man, saw him turn and then stop to wait for him. The bleating grew louder as the dog crept along the flock, quiet and calm one minute, then racing after the wandering ones the next.

"Hello," the man said. "You ride from Pueblo?"

"Yes. I'm going to Santa Fe. You have the road blocked with all these sheep."

"I am sorry, but there are many sheep. They take up much room."

"Where are you taking them?"

"To the grass in the mountains."

"A little early, isn't it? There's still a lot of snow up there."

"It will take many weeks to climb to where we are going. Why do you not rest awhile? I will take a smoke with you until the sheep pass and clear the road."

"I'm kind of in a hurry. Did you see three men ride past you on the road?"

"I saw them, from a long way off. They were in a hurry, too. They are friends of yours?"

Lew shook his head.

"No. One of them murdered his family in Pueblo."

"You are a lawman?"

Lew hesitated. What was he? A vigilante? An outlaw?

He shook his head again.

"No. I seek justice."

"Ah, justice. There is no justice in this world, my friend."

"You are a Mexican?"

"No. I am a Basque. My people are from the Pyrenees, the mountains that border Spain. But I speak the Spanish. I am called Joe Eramouspe, and you?"

"Lew Wetzel," he said, unwilling to speak his surname to a stranger. He thought about that for a brief moment. He was being deceptive, he knew, so maybe he was an outlaw, or thinking like one.

"That sounds like a German name," Eramouspe said. "Are you German?"

"American."

"I mean your family."

"I reckon."

"Very fine people, the Germans. Will you wait for the sheep to pass?"

"Would it bother them for me to ride through?" Lew looked around. The herd was very large. It would take him a couple of hours to ride around it.

"I can make you a path. With my boys and my dog."

"What kind of dog is that?"

"That is what they call a border collie. Her name is Lacy. She is very smart. A good dog."

"Yes, I can see that."

Eramouspe put two fingers in his mouth and let out a sharp whistle. The two boys looked over at him and then started wading through the sheep, coming his way. The dog snapped at the sheep, turned tail, and ran toward Joe.

"Would you like something to drink? My wife has tea and a Mexican drink she makes with bananas and beer, called *tepache*. The tea and the *tepache* are very cool. She keeps them in the ollas. It will not make you drunk, but it will put a little fire in your blood, eh?"

Lew laughed.

"I think I've got enough fire in my blood, thanks. I won't have tea, either, thank you. I want to be on my way."

"If you catch up to these men, what will you do?"

Before Lew could answer, the two boys came up. Joe spoke to them, then they called to Lacy and she followed them. They began clearing a path through the sheep, right where the road cut through the flock.

What would he do about those men? Lew couldn't say for sure. He had only caught a glimpse of Wayne Smith, but he was sure he could recognize him if he saw him again. He did not know who the other two men were, but they could be trouble. It was three against one.

"I guess I'll turn the one man in to the law up in Santa Fe," Lew said. "There might be a U.S. marshal come along directly. He's after one of the men, too. And he might ask about me."

"Is he after you, as well, eh?"

"We know each other," Lew said.

"I see. Well, there is your path, Lew Wetzel. Go with God, eh?"

"Thanks, Joe. I wish you luck with your sheep."

"We will fatten them in the mountains and then sell them in Denver. Then, we go to New Mexico."

"Santa Fe?"

"No, a little town. You would not know it. My brother says there is trouble there. I want to help him if I can."

"He raises sheep, too?"

"Yes. It is very hard to raise sheep there. His name is Ben Eramouspe."

"What's the name of the town where he lives?"

"Socorro. Do you know what that name means?"

Lew shook his head.

"It is like when you give aid to a traveler. Help him when he is tired or has hunger."

"Sounds like a nice place."

Joe's face darkened.

"It once was a good place, yes."

"Not now?"

"My brother, he does not say what the trouble is, but he is very worried. Or he would not write such things to me. I know there is much trouble there."

"I hope it all works out for Ben and you, Joe. *Buena suerte.*"

"Ah, you speak the Spanish. That is good. If you go to New Mexico, there is much Spanish spoken there."

"I know a little."

"You had best go while your way is cleared, Lew Wetzel."

"Yes. Thank you, Joe."

Lew rode Ruben slowly so he would not disturb the sheep. The boys waved at him as he passed. The dog worked ahead of them, pushing sheep to the left and right. When he looked back, the path had closed and the sheep were moving toward Fountain Creek, a slow, undulating pile of wool. When he looked back toward Joe, the Basque was waving good-bye to him.

He wondered if they would ever meet again.

The wind came up and the horse tracks started to blur. But the riders were no longer moving fast. It grew warm, but was still fairly cool as the breeze swept down off the snow-capped mountains. Ruben shied at a diamondback, and that probably saved Lew's life.

Ahead, he saw an orange flash. A moment later something whizzed past his ear, sounding like an angry hornet.

Then, he heard the report.

A rifle shot.

It had come from a jumble of rocks just to the right of the road.

Someone was shooting at him.

He did not know who or why.

But he put the spurs to Ruben and rode into a shallow arroyo just as another shot rang out, sounding like a bullwhip cracking. He heard the lead whine as the bullet caromed off a rock near where he had been a split second before.

The road to Santa Fe was turning mighty dangerous.

3

LEW JERKED HIS RIFLE FROM ITS BOOT AND SLID FROM THE saddle. He pushed Ruben to the lowest point of the arroyo, where his head would not be seen, and tapped his knees. It was a trick he had taught the horse, to lie down like a camel when his knees were tapped. Ruben folded up his forelegs and crumpled to the ground, obedient as any well-trained dog, and a lot smarter, Lew figured.

He crawled cautiously up the bank until he reached a point just below the rim. There, he waited. He took off his hat and laid it beside him. He peered over the edge until he could see the jumble of rocks where he had seen the powder flash when the rifle first exploded.

The bottom of the arroyo was damp—still wet from the snowmelt, he imagined. Plants grew along the sides, cholla, nopal, greasewood. There was brush on the top and he hid behind a prickly pear, peering through its wide, flat, spiny leaves. He saw movement among the rocks and made out a human form scrambling to another position. He eased his rifle up and poked it through the cactus, levering a cartridge into the chamber.

He lay very still. He knew he could not be seen if he did not move. Not from that distance, a good two hundred yards.

He had learned that from the western jackrabbit. When he had first seen one, he watched it run, then stop on a piece of ground that matched its color. The rabbit had turned almost invisible. He watched it for a long time. It sat there as if frozen, and Lew thought it was a good survival trick, something he might use himself one day.

He saw the sun flash on something among the rocks and he knew right away what it was.

"So, that's how Smith knew I was coming," he said softly.

He stayed perfectly still, knowing that one of the men, probably Smith, was using a pair of field glasses to look for him. The flash appeared each time the man in the rocks moved the binoculars to another angle.

Lew put the rifle slowly to his shoulder and sighted down the barrel. He was already uncomfortable, lying there, rocks pressing into his flesh. No telling how long they were willing to wait him out. But he was not going to be made a prisoner by these three.

The lenses of the binoculars flashed again, two quick bursts of light. Lew drew a bead on the flashes, allowed for windage and bullet drop, and squeezed the trigger. The rifle boomed, butted against his shoulder. Smoke and fire belched from the barrel of the Winchester '73. He saw the bullet strike the top of a rock and spew sparks. He heard someone yell.

He pulled the rifle back off the ridge and ducked down, then rolled a few feet away to another position. He heard a shot, followed by another, and dirt spewed up in front of the cactus where he had been.

"Pretty good shots," he said as falling dirt rattled atop his hat brim.

Another shot rang out and kicked up to the right of where he had been. The men in the rocks had guessed wrong.

A moment later, another rifle cracked and a bullet plowed a furrow closer to where he now lay. They were trying to find him, maybe hoping for a lucky shot.

The sky was a soft periwinkle blue, and little puffs of white clouds floated serenely above the stark landscape to the east. Huge white thunderheads slowly rose from behind the range of snowcapped mountains. As Lew had come to know, the mountains produced their own weather. It could be calm and beautiful one moment, then those giant thunderheads would rise up from some distant valley and turn black, pregnant with rain or snow. It was that kind of day that made anyone with a weather eye very wary.

More movement in the rocks. He saw two men scramble for different positions behind the small outcroppings. Below, he saw the flick of a horse's tail and knew their mounts were not far away. They must have wanted him pretty bad to go to all that trouble, he thought. They picked a perfect place for an ambush. On the other side of the rocks, the ground sloped downward, and to the north, a short dip and then a rise. Anyone wanting to get away fast and lose their silhouette would have only a short distance to ride before they would be out of sight. But Smith didn't know this country. He was from Missouri. One or both of the other men must be familiar with the terrain, Lew reasoned. But who were they? And why was Smith riding with them after murdering his wife and kids?

Lew waited, concentrating on the closest man. He knew right where he was, and he knew he would have to show some of himself when he attempted to make another shot. The flashes were not as close together now, but someone up there was searching for him mighty hard.

Lew stretched his right arm to full length, just below the rim and out of sight of the men who were looking for him. He was tired of waiting. He slid his hand up over the edge and touched a sagebrush. He shook it so that the top of it moved back and forth. Then he withdrew his hand and gripped the rifle, leaning over the receiver until he had the front and rear sights lined up.

The man closest to him rose up and took a bead on the sagebrush. Just as he pulled the trigger, Lew fired his Winchester. He saw the man jerk backward and drop his rifle. The sagebrush quivered as the man's bullet tore through it, severing some of the stalks.

Then two men rose up, crouching, showing their backsides. Lew levered another cartridge into the firing chamber and cracked off a shot. He dusted a rock between the two men and he knew they were peppered by rock splinters. The two men scrambled down the other side. Lew fired another shot and heard the bullet whine as it caromed off a rock. The men were no longer there.

A few seconds later, he saw them burst from behind the pile of rocks and the ridge, riding hell-bent-for-leather to the east. He started to shoot again, but decided not to waste a bullet. They were hightailing it by then, and soon disappeared after they cut north.

He heard a moan and saw an arm waving in the air up in the rocks where he had downed the man who had shot at him.

"Help, for God's sake. Wayne, come back."

"He won't be back just yet," Lew said, and slid down the bank. He rammed two cartridges into the rifle's magazine and shoved it in its boot, then climbed aboard Ruben. He turned the horse and bolted up the slope and out of the arroyo. Lew put him into a gallop, his eyes scanning the rocks for any glint of metal, but all he saw was that arm stuck up in the air, waving back and forth.

He climbed off his horse and drew his pistol. Then he wended his way through the rocks and stood over the wounded man. The man's eyes were filled with fresh tears and all of the color had gone out of his face. He looked as if he had swallowed a can of paste and it had exuded out through his pores. There was blood on his shirt, and Lew saw a coil of intestine oozing from the hole in his belly. It glistened in the sun like a newborn snake, or a large oily worm.

"You Zane?" the man groaned.

Lew nodded.

"You kill Wayne and K.C.?"

The man's pistol was still in its holster, but he started sliding a bloody hand toward it.

"You're gut-shot," Lew said. "You don't have too long to live. If you put a hand on that pistol, your time will be even shorter."

"No, I reckon I don't need no revenge right now. You got me good."

The man's words were labored, an odd resonance to them considering he was slowly bleeding to death and the blowflies were already at his exposed intestine. He probably didn't feel them walking around on it, sucking up all the juice on the surface.

"Who are you?" Lew asked.

"Why?"

"I want to know why you were taking potshots at me. You got folks, maybe I'll let them know so they can come and get you."

The man shook his head.

"Nobody would come," he said. "Name's Turner. Bill Turner. Not that it matters none."

"Why were you shooting at me, Turner?"

"Wayne said you'd be coming down the road, a-chasin' him. Said you was sweet on his woman."

"He tell you he murdered his wife?"

"No."

"Did he tell you he killed his children, too?"

"I reckon not. Why would he do that?"

"He had them insured. Means to collect a bounty on them."

Turner swore under his breath, of which he had very little left at that point. His face turned even pastier, grayer.

"Wayne told us you kilt his wife and kids."

"You believe him?"

"Yep. Me'n Wayne go back a long ways."

"Who's the other man with Smith? He a friend of yours?"

"Why, sure. K.C., we call him. Me'n K.C. been pards since . . . a real long time. I didn't think he'd run out on me like that, though. Wayne, neither."

"Wayne seems in a real big hurry. Where were you all going, anyway?"

"Denver."

"I thought Smith was going to Santa Fe."

"He is. After he takes care of business in Denver. Then, he's goin' to Santa Fe. But why should I tell you what for, Zane? You probably sent me to hell already."

"You tell me what I want to know, Turner, and I'll try and plug that hole for you. You might just get over that belly-ache."

Turner looked down at his stomach. He winced when he saw the blood. There wasn't a lot of it, because he had pinched the biggest part of the hole closed. Now he pressed on the piece of intestine with his thumb and it disappeared. There was the smell, though, and Lew knew that his intestines were probably torn up inside. Turner would not live long.

"What can you do for me, Zane?"

"I can make some mud to clog up that hole. Bullet go through, or is it still inside?"

"I think it went on through. I heard it chink on a rock after I got hit. You run a .44 through that barrel?"

"Yeah. That's the caliber of my Winchester."

"Felt like a damned sledgehammer when it hit me. I figured a .44."

"What's Wayne up to, anyway?"

"We was meetin' up with some boys in Denver. Payroll job. Big money. Then we was going to light out for Santa Fe. That Wayne, he's always got big ideas. We helped him back in Bolivar, Missouri. He give us the tip, and we knocked over a bank. Got away clean. A right smart boy, that Wayne. Hey, this is startin' to hurt. You gonna do somethin' for me?"

"Yeah. In a minute. Wayne have a place to hole up in Santa Fe?"

"He says so. I don't know where, though. He don't tell me and K.C. everything."

"Some of what he told you is a damned lie," Lew said. "I didn't kill his wife and kids."

"You say."

"Yeah, I say. Do you know where he's going to knock over this payroll in Denver?"

"Brown Palace Hotel, he said. Least that's where we're all going to meet."

"How many men is he meeting in Denver?"

"Just two. Don't know their names. They're from Bolivar, he said."

"Missouri boys, eh?"

"Yep. K.C. ain't from Missouri, though. He's from Taos."

"Too bad you're all going to Denver. Wayne will have to double back and come this same way to go down to Santa Fe."

"Yep."

"Maybe I should wait him out right here," Lew said.

"I'd take it kindly if you could stay with me while I ride this out. I'm feelin' real bad, Zane. Kinda dizzy like, and you're startin' to swim around like a fish."

Turner's eyes watered again and he tried to focus his eyes.

Lew had a hunch Turner wouldn't last much longer. He wondered how much more information he could get out of the man, and if what he had heard was reliable.

"What's in Santa Fe for Wayne? He got a woman there?"

"A man he knows. Says he can put us into some big money. Gold, silver maybe."

"Know the man's name?"

Turner shook his head.

"Wayne don't tell us a whole lot, like I said."

Turner's breath was starting to get thready. He gulped in air, and when he let it out, he wheezed as if his lungs were filling up with sand. Or blood. The bullet Lew had put in him had probably missed his liver, but he knew it had sure torn the hell out of his guts. The smell was getting worse. A shadow passed over Turner's face. Lew glanced up and saw a buzzard flap its wings high in the sky. It turned and began to circle. He saw another one out of the corner of his eye.

"You do any praying, Turner?" Lew asked.

"Nope. Never did much. Why?"

"If you're ever going to, now might be the time. I don't think there's anything I can do for you."

"You mean I'm gonna die? Oh, shit."

"I reckon. We're all going to die. You a little sooner than some."

"Damn you, Zane. You're a heartless bastard."

"I wouldn't be calling anyone names right now, if I were you, Turner. Save your breath. You'll need it."

Turner struggled, trying to rise. His hand stayed away from his pistol, but he couldn't make it. He collapsed back down, and now there was a rattle in his throat.

"I c-can't breathe," he stammered.

The sound of retreating hoofbeats had long since faded, but Lew could still hear them in memory. Smith and K.C. were getting away. He might never catch up to them. He wondered if he should just let them go and head for Santa Fe. It was none of his business what Smith did in Denver. Except he had killed the woman Lew had fallen in love with, and kids he cared for.

Turner's eyes frosted over. He gasped for air and stretched an arm toward Zane.

He started to utter something, but he never got it out. He let out a rattling sigh and then collapsed. His eyes closed, and when Lew bent down to listen, he heard no breathing.

A buzzard landed on the highest rock behind them, flapped its wings slowly, cocked its head.

Lew stood up.

"Too bad, Turner," he said. "You rode with the wrong man at the wrong time."

There was no answer, of course. There would never be an answer. Turner was dead.

Lew looked down at his hands. There was no blood on them, but he could feel the stain burning into his flesh like the mark of Cain. He wondered if he was cursed, somehow, destined to go on killing and killing and killing . . .

He drew a breath and holstered the Colt. Then he wiped the backs of both hands, for no reason. For no reason at all.

4

THE DECISION WAS TAKEN OUT OF LEW'S HANDS ONCE HE WAS mounted on Ruben. He heard the soft thunder of hoofbeats and drew back behind the jagged pyramid of rocks. The sound grew louder, more thunderous, and it seemed he could feel the ground shake beneath his horse. But he knew that was only an illusion. The horses were too far away, the ground too solid.

One of the buzzards squawked, and another lit on the rocks just above where the body of Bill Turner lay.

Lew stood up in the stirrups and peered over toward the road. The hoofbeats stopped, and he saw a dozen or so men, all heavily armed, rein to a stop. He recognized Blackhawk at the head of the column. He sat there, one arm raised to call a halt. As Lew watched, Blackhawk rode around in a circle, leaning over to look at the ground. The marshal hesitated, then looked toward the pile of rocks, saw the buzzards. The birds were flapping and hopping around, squawking low. More landed, and more were circling overhead, spiraling in lazy circles on invisible currents of air.

He saw Blackhawk move his lips and gesture as he spoke to the men on horseback. In a moment, he was riding toward where Lew sat his horse. Lew waited, wary. But if the marshal had wanted to take him, put him under arrest, he reasoned, he would have brought the bunch of men with him when he rode toward Lew.

"Zane?" Blackhawk called out.

"I'm here, Marshal."

"What the hell's going on?"

"There's a dead man up there in those rocks. He tried to kill me. A man named Bill Turner."

"I know who he is. He's wanted for robbery back in Missouri. One of Wayne Smith's waddies. You just can't stay away from being a vigilante, can you?"

"He shot at me. Wayne rode off with another feller."

"Know who that was?"

"Turner said he was called K.C. That's all I know. I thought you said Smith was going to Santa Fe."

"That's what we heard. Looks like I was wrong. Know where he's going, by any chance?"

"Turner said Denver. A payroll robbery. Then he's going to Santa Fe for something else. I don't know what."

"That's good information. If you weren't a wanted man, I'd think about deputizing you."

Lew snorted. Another buzzard flapped down onto the rocks. He could hear the birds tearing at Turner's flesh. He knew they'd take out the eyes first. Blackhawk looked up, saw the birds hopping around.

"What you got over there, all those men?"

"A posse. The constable, the sheriff, some deputies. They want Smith pretty bad. So do I."

"I don't want him to get away with what he did, Blackhawk."

"He won't. You know anything more that might help us?"

"Turner said they were going to meet at the Brown Palace Hotel."

"Yeah, makes sense. It's brand-new. Just opened. Well, that gives us more than we had. Thanks. What are you going to do?"

"I'm thinking on it."

"Want my advice?"

"It's free, isn't it?"

Blackhawk smiled. "Don't go to Denver. Go someplace else. I ought to put you in irons right now, but Smith is more important. I'll get to you later."

"Then I won't tell you where I'm going," Lew said.

"I know where you're going, Zane."

"Oh?"

"I'd bet Santa Fe. In case we don't get Smith. You'll be there, waiting for him."

"Good luck, Blackhawk. I'll see you by and by, maybe."

Blackhawk touched a hand to his hat and turned his horse.

"You take care, Lew," he said, using his first name for a change.

"You, too, Horatio. Those sheep still blocking the road back there?"

"Nope. They're all lined up along Fountain Creek, guzzling that muddy water. Ride careful, and if you follow my advice, you'll give up being a vigilante. You'll stay out of trouble, if you're smart. And you'll live a heap longer. Be seeing you, Lew."

Lew did not say good-bye. He watched Blackhawk join the other men, then turned Ruben and rode behind the rocks. He wanted to be on his way in case the marshal changed his mind and came back with some help to take him into custody.

He put Ruben into a gallop and headed south toward Santa Fe, leaving the gabbling buzzards and the posse behind.

Lew skirted Pueblo with its grimy smokestacks and clanking machinery, taking to the lonesome high desert where he could be alone with his thoughts. He missed Carol and what might have been before her husband cut her life short. But now he began to think of Seneca again. He owed her an explanation, a kindness for what she had gone through herself because of him. She might want to know where he was and what he was doing, but he'd have to be careful about how much he told her. Still, he missed her, and as he rode through the desolate land in the shadow of the Rockies with their towering spires, passing Spanish Peaks and marveling at nature's sculpture, past mesas that echoed of muffled drumbeats, visions of smoke signals from some ancient war party, and the majestic buttes that looked almost like man-made structures, he thought of Seneca and even saw her lovely face, her soft hair, her lithe figure. And it seemed he could hear her laugh, see her smile, her lips curving like a Valentine as they sat on her front porch, the air perfumed with the scent of cedars and wisteria.

He missed the Ozarks, too—the gentle green hills, the dark, steep hollows where squirrels scurried among the fallen leaves and deer wandered the hardwoods, feeding on acorns. The poke would be growing about now, he thought, and the redbuds all abloom, the dogwoods flowering white lights in the dense green. Soon the hummingbirds would return, and if his mother were still alive she would have put out for them sugared water that she had dyed red. The wild strawberries would be pushing up through the leaves that had sheltered them from the cold air all winter, and his father's asparagus would soon break through the soil and begin to grow tall and slender and succulent.

The following day, Raton Pass loomed ahead, and he took to the road, the memory of Pueblo and the horror there fading as he closed in on the mountains, shook off the night chill. It would be a steep climb, he knew, and cold up there, but he had a warm jacket and could make fire if he ran into a late snow squall.

He had been on the main road to Santa Fe a little more than an hour, with the hills now on both sides of him, when he heard the whipcrack of a rifle shot, followed by the popping sound of pistols. He thought he saw a puff of smoke rise up some three or four hundred yards ahead, but he was not sure.

He loosened the pistol in its holster and made sure he could pull the Winchester from its boot. There was a rise ahead, and the shooting had come from just beyond there. It grew quiet. And then, as he drew closer to the top of the rise, he heard a sound that made his blood turn chill.

A woman screamed, her voice high-pitched and laden with terror.

And then Lew was engulfed in a silence so deep, he thought he had grown deaf.

He topped the rise, his pistol drawn, his thumb on the hammer.

The woman screamed again, and Lew's blood curdled with ice.

5

THERE WERE THREE MEN WRESTLING WITH A WOMAN. AN-
other man lay motionless on the ground next to an over-
turned Red River cart hooked to a skittery mule that was
braying and kicking out both hind legs as if trying to get rid
of the wagon so it could run away. Three horses stood
nearby, hitched to some stunted pines that grew alongside
the road. The woman screamed again, and Lew hammered
back the Colt and fired a shot into the air.

He raced Ruben down the slope to the bottom.

"The next shot will take off one of your heads," Lew said.
"You let that woman go. Now."

One of the men looked up at him and drew his pistol. He
started to bring it up. Lew leaned over the side of the horse,
took aim, and fired a shot. The man clutched his chest and
staggered backward, blood flowering like a crimson rose on
his chest.

The mule broke and made a dash up the road. The men at-
tacking the woman both drew their pistols and started shooting at Lew. He ducked and reined Ruben into a tight turn as
the men scrambled over to their horses. Bullets sizzled the
air over his head, and one whistled past his ear with an angry
whine that sent shivers up his spine.

Lew sat up straight and hauled in on the reins. Ruben planted his hind feet and clawed the ground with his front hooves to keep from sliding back onto the road. Lew fired at the nearest man, who was turning his horse, trying to flee. The Colt thundered in his hand, the hot powder from blow-back prickling his face, but he saw the man stiffen as a small puff of dust lifted off the back of his vest.

The remaining man turned and fired at Lew. But he was on the run, and his shot went wild. He shouted something to his partner and they both disappeared into the pines bordering the road.

Lew rode down, wary, listening to the sound of retreating hoofbeats. He heard rocks breaking loose and rolling downhill, the crash and snap of broken limbs as the two men made their escape.

When he was close to the sobbing woman, he waited until the noises faded away, then holstered his pistol and swung down out of the saddle. He tied Ruben to a scrub pine on the other side of the road and walked over to the man he had seen lying there. He stooped down and floated his hand over the man's closed mouth, his nostrils. He looked at his chest. He was not moving. He was not breathing. The man had flecks of gray in his sideburns and in his moustache. His hair was turning snowy, too, but he did not look old. His eyes were closed, and there was blood all over the front of his linsey-woolsey shirt. Lew saw the dark hole just above his belly. There was blood at the corners of the man's mouth and on his chin, but he must have died pretty quick, or there would have been more.

He stood up and walked over to the woman, who was now crumpled in a heap, her head in her hands. She was sobbing deeply, and he saw that she was much younger than the man. Her hands were small and girlish, and there were flecks of blood on her plain cotton dress. Spatter, he believed, from being close to the dead man when he was shot.

"Miss, or ma'am. What happened here? Can you tell me?"

"Is—is he dead? My pa?"

"The man on the ground? He's your pa?"

She nodded, still sobbing.

"Yes," Lew said. "He is dead. I'm real sorry."

She looked up at him then, her eyes red-rimmed, bleary, her face streaked with tears. Her body shook as she tried to control the sobbing.

"They—they were . . . those men . . . those rude, mean, men."

"Do you know them?"

She nodded, and then her eyes got wild. They opened wide as if she were looking into the face of terror, as if she wanted to scream at the top of her lungs.

"No, I mean, they . . . they looked at me. In town. They said things. Bad things. But I didn't know they would . . ."

She broke down again. She squeezed her eyes shut, real tight, as if she were making fists with her lids. Tears eked out anyway, and she shook all over as she tried to stifle her sobs.

"Ma'am, are you all right?"

His words seemed to jar her back to reality. She looked over at the dead man, then at Lew.

"Dead? Are you sure?"

"Yes, ma'am. I'm right sorry."

"He—he's my father. Oh dear." Then she looked over at the man Zane had shot. She shuddered.

"He was the worst," she said. "His name is Calvin, I think. Calvin Weems. Yes, that's him. He—he tried to get me to go in the hotel with him in Pueblo. He—he's the one who shot my father. Just rode up and shot him. Oh, oh, I can't bear it."

She started crying again, and Lew stood there, helpless against her paroxysm of grief, unable to find words of comfort at such a dark time in her life.

"You want me to bury him? I don't have a shovel, but I can dig a shallow grave and cover him with rocks so the critters won't get at him. I mean, you don't want to just leave him out here for the buzzards and coyotes, ma'am."

She stopped crying, and he helped her to her feet. Her dress was torn and there were dirty smudges on her neck and face. He noticed her fingernails were broken. So, she had fought hard.

"Do you know who the other two men were? The ones with Calvin Weems?"

She nodded. "I heard their names in town. They're bad men. Robbers, I'm sure."

"Yes'm."

"The tall thin one is Fritz Gunther. They called him Fritzie. The other one, the short one, they called Hatfield. Billy Hatfield, I think."

"You might want to look around and find a nice resting place for your father. And maybe go through his pockets and get anything you want to keep."

He left her alone while she bent down and kissed her father on the forehead, then on the lips. He watched as she removed his money pouch from under his belt and a small prayer book from his shirt pocket. She got up and walked over to the side of the road and looked both ways, then stepped into the scraggly timber, brushing past the scrub pine and skirting the prickly pear that grew on the hillside.

Giant fluffy white clouds floated up over the rimrock above, glided out over the road, blocking the sun. Thunderheads, born from some far valley deep in the Rockies, kept billowing out toward the vast plain, casting him and everything in shadow. He walked to the slain man's horse and looked at the brand. He didn't recognize it. He went through the saddlebags and found .44/40 pistol and rifle cartridges, a cloth sack full of hardtack, another with dried beef jerky, a small tin of coffee, an empty airtight with the closed end blackened—probably what he cooked his coffee in—matches, a can of peaches, and a spare canteen that was full of liquid, water or whiskey, he guessed. There was a rifle in the boot and another canteen dangling from the saddlehorn. At least the woman would have a horse to ride if she wanted to find her cart and mule.

"Down here," she called, and Lew stepped away from the sorrel gelding and walked down through the scrub. She stood in a grassy spot shaded by a large rock that was flat on one side. He stepped on the grass and thought he might dig into it a couple of inches.

"This'll do," he said, and knelt down. He took his knife from its scabbard and stuck the point into the earth and made a large oval to mark the dig. She watched him, her eyes wet with tears.

"What's your name?" she asked. "I don't even know your name."

"Lew," he said.

"Just Lew?"

"Lew, ah, Wetzel. And yours?"

"Marylynn. Marylynn Baxter. My father's name—it's Rex William. Rex William Baxter."

"I'll bring him down directly. I can't go very deep. There's hard rock under the grass. You might want to start gathering rocks to put over him. Just line them up by that big rock yonder. Give you something to do, and we'll need them."

"Thank you, Lew. You're very considerate."

He kept digging, and when he had a sufficient chunk of earth removed, he got up and walked back up to the road. He could hear the chunking sound of rocks as she gathered and dropped them in a pile.

More clouds barreled over the ridges, and the temperature began to drop a degree or two. He lifted the body of Rex Baxter and slung it over his shoulder and started back. He had looked at the country below the spot where Marylynn had chosen to bury her father, and it was rugged, filled with rolling hills and empty as a hollowed-out gourd. Plenty of places for those killers to hide, but he didn't think they were anywhere watching them. No telling where they had gone, but they had some choices. They could ride out on the plain, go back to Pueblo, or continue on over the pass.

Marylynn was still gathering rocks when he returned with the body of her father. He set him down in the shallow grave he had dug, put the man's booted feet together, crossed his hands over his chest, and made sure his eyes were closed.

"I wish we had a blanket to put over him," she said. She searched her pockets for a kerchief or some piece of cloth to put over his face.

"You might not want to look," Lew said.

A hawk floated past them, skimming the air on wafting currents, its head moving back and forth, its wings outstretched.

Marylynn didn't see it, but Lew watched it float down toward the plain, following some invisible river of air.

Lew untied the bandanna from around his neck. It was grimy and soggy from sweat, but he laid it over Rex Baxter's face while Marylynn watched. Then he began to throw the dirt he had dug over the body, starting at the feet to give her time to look away when he got to the face. He was surprised when she helped him place rocks over her father's corpse, and he knew it must have been hard for her.

When they were finished, there was a mound of rocks marking the grave and covering Baxter's body.

"I don't have a cross to put here," Lew said, feeling awkward.

"Daddy don't need no cross. He was a God-fearing man, put store by the Holy Bible. You rest easy, Daddy," she said. "I love you."

Lew was touched by her words. He had taken his hat off to show respect, and he put it back on, felt the nakedness of his neck with the bandanna gone. But he had another in his saddlebags. It was fairly clean, perhaps a bit dusty.

They walked back up to the road together. He helped her through the rocks and brush. He was surprised to find that she wasn't as frail as she looked. There was steel in her arms, and he knew she was probably used to hard work back wherever she had come from.

"You'll ride that outlaw's horse," Lew said.

"What about him? Shouldn't we . . ."

"Bury him?"

"Well, yes."

He helped her into the saddle and saw that she knew what to do when she picked up the reins and held the horse in check.

"The buzzards and critters will take care of him. Don't you fret yourself about that no-good."

She gave him a sharp look, and he turned away, walked to his horse. His hands were sore from the digging and handling the rocks. He had a nick or two that had drawn blood, but those would heal fast. He mounted up, turned his horse toward her.

"You know, Lew," she said, "I was very touched by your giving up your bandanna to cover my daddy, and when you took your hat off, I knew you were a caring man. But that dead man there was a human. You have a cold spot in you that I don't quite understand. I'm sorry."

"Yes'm," he said. "I reckon I do have a cold spot in me. Truth is, that man killed your daddy, and he doesn't deserve a decent burial. Maybe that's the justice spot in me, small as it is."

"Justice? What do you know about justice?" she asked.

Her question surprised him.

"Not much, Marylynn. Just that it seems to be scarce as hairs on a frog."

They rode toward the pass, neither speaking. By late afternoon, there was a chill in the air and the sun had vanished under the thick carpet of clouds that were turning dark on their undersides. Lew was watching every crook in the road, riding ahead toward every rise, wondering if the two men who got away might be waiting to jump them somewhere up ahead. He saw that the dead man had tied a slicker behind the cantle of his saddle, and he knew that Marylynn might have to put it on before the day was done.

The light began to fade and there was no sign of the mule or cart for all those slow miles as the road climbed toward Raton Pass, which was smothered in black clouds.

And, no matter where Lew looked, there wasn't a sign of life.

6

THEY RODE INTO CLOUDS, LEW AND MARYLYNN, MIST SLICKING their faces, dark clouds as far as the eye could see. The road was steep and rocky, the footing hard on the horses with their iron shoes wet and the rocks slippery as if they had been slimed with oil. But Marylynn never complained. There was no sign of her cart, nor were any of her goods strewn along the way. The underbellies of the clouds had darkened even more, and there was the subtle tang of rain in the air. They could taste it. They could feel it, but they hadn't heard so much as a mutter of thunder, nor had lightning bolted from the black sky.

Lew saw talus slopes rising steep to the right of the road, looking like the ruins of some ancient citadel, and tall pines shrouded in brume, as if they grew not from the ground but from the sky. The road was littered with wagon and animal tracks, yet they saw no other parties making the journey either way. A bad sign. Perhaps experienced travelers knew better than to approach the high pass late in the day and made their camps well below the place where the road steepened.

He saw the flash an instant before he heard the whipcrack of the rifle. He shoved Marylynn to one side, which may have saved her life. The shot came from somewhere up ahead on the right slope, but he could not tell from where, exactly.

"Hug your horse," he yelled to her and grabbed her reins just short of the bit and jerked the animal off to the left. He hunched over himself as another rifle shot pierced the stillness with a resounding snap. He heard the whine of a bullet as it caromed off a rock. Sparks flew and the shards stung his horse's legs so that it bucked and lashed out with its hind legs at an unseen enemy.

"Easy, boy," Lew said, and rode his horse and Marylynn's into the trees and brush below the road. Two more shots followed in rapid succession and he heard the bullets cut swaths through the trees over their heads.

They were firing blind now.

"Lew, I'm scared," she said when he halted her horse.

"You stay here with the horses. Dismount and stay low, behind some rocks if you can."

"What are you going to do?"

"I'm going to sneak up there and see if I can find whoever's shooting at us. I may be a while."

"Be careful," she said.

Lew pulled his rifle from its scabbard and slid from the saddle. He saw some boulders stacked in a pile where another, larger rock had stopped some long-ago landslide. He pointed to it and gestured for Marylynn to take cover there. He showed her where to tie the horses.

He saw her pull the outlaw's rifle from its boot and was surprised. She lit down and tied up the horses, then crept to a spot behind the rocks. He saw her cock the lever-action Winchester and breathed a sigh of relief.

At least, he thought, Marylynn could defend herself.

He hunched low and crabbed across the road, cocking his rifle on the run. He made noise with his boots, dislodging gravel, but he didn't think the sound would carry. When he reached the other side, he began climbing. He wanted to get above the two shooters. He was convinced there were two, since the rifle shots had sounded slightly different. That was confirmed when two more quick shots exploded ahead of him. He heard the swish of the bullets tearing through brush and pine needles. He started angling toward the spot where he had first glimpsed the orange flash.

It was rugged going. The slope was steep and rocky, covered with tangled brush. He tried not to dislodge rocks, but some did roll downhill. Again he hoped the sound would not carry far enough so that the shooters could hear him coming.

It was quiet for a while, and Lew kept climbing and angling toward where he thought the bushwhackers might be.

There was a talus slope blocking his way. If he stepped into it, the loose rock could start moving and slide him down to the road. He'd be helpless and an easy target. He would have to go above it, and that would take time. He grabbed a bush and pulled himself up another foot or two. The slope was steeper than it had looked from below.

He climbed higher, then realized that he'd be in the open during the last stretch before he reached the stunted pines above the strewn talus. He listened before moving on, listened and waited until his breathing returned to normal. Then he edged up the slope, crabbing sideways to keep from dislodging rocks or losing ground because of a misstep.

He grabbed the trunk of a wind-stunted pine and hauled himself up above the loose shale. He crawled behind the tree and caught his breath. A rock dislodged below him and started rolling. It gathered speed and then made a lot of racket as it tumbled downhill toward the road. He drew one of his legs up.

That's when he heard the rifle bark again. The bullet struck just above the spot where his leg had been, ripping a furrow in the earth not a foot away from his hiding place. Lew's heart felt as if someone had squeezed it, and his stomach roiled with winged insects. Two more shots zeroed in on him, and he knew he had to move even higher. The tree was so small it afforded him little protection. Sooner or later, one of those boys would wing him and he'd be in a heap of trouble.

He couldn't see the two men, but he had marked where the shots had come from and had a pretty good idea where they were. No chance for him to take a shot, though. He had to get out of there, and quick, before the two men flanked him or rushed him.

The quiet was unnerving. He expected to hear probing shots from the two men, but their rifles were silent. He scrambled to higher ground, traversed the most dangerous stretch, and started looking for the rocks that marked the hiding place of the bushwhackers.

Lew dropped to his belly when he caught sight of the spot where the two men had lain in ambush. He was quiet, but one or both of them must have seen him, because the stillness exploded with the crackling sound of two rifle shots very close together. The brush above Lew rattled as bullets tore through the leaves. He heard the brittle sound of branches breaking. The two rifles fired again and bullets plowed gouges in the earth just below him. Dirt spattered his face and he rolled downhill a few feet and took up a position behind a small boulder. Bullets spanged against it and he knew the two men had him cold.

Lew started digging a hole, clawing his fingers through the dirt so he could nestle still lower and try for a shot. Otherwise, he was a dead man.

He finished digging a small depression as the shots continued on a sporadic basis, bullets thumping into the ground all around him. He decided he'd better adopt a ruse, or they would bracket him and rush him before he had a chance to defend himself.

When the next bullet came close, Lew cried out, as if he were wounded. He continued to dig and then slunk into the hollow he had formed with his bare hands. He laid the rifle out in front of him, levered a shell into the chamber, and waited.

"We got him," one of the men said. There was glee in his voice.

"Sounded like it," the other man said.

"Let's go finish him off."

"Wait."

Lew saw a head poke from behind the rocks. It would have been a snap shot, and he didn't want to risk it. He would wait until both men showed themselves and then try to bring them both down.

He waited, listening.

Then, he began to moan loudly.

"Help me," he whined.

"He's wounded," one of the men said. "Pretty bad, I'd say."

"Maybe. I don't trust the bastard."

Lew moaned some more, then gave out a loud groan and what he hoped was a rattling sigh. He gurgled in his throat, and then was quiet.

"We got the bastard," one of the men said.

Lew heard a rustling from the other side of the rocky outcropping.

One of the men stood up.

Then, from the road, he heard a rifle shot. Before he could squeeze the trigger, the man grabbed for his shoulder and then fell to the ground. He rolled a few yards. The other man stood up, just a little, but enough so that Lew had a shot. He lined up the front blade in the center of the buckhorn rear sight and gently squeezed the trigger. The Winchester barked and spat lead and flame, sparks flittering like fireflies in the low clouds.

"Ah," the man said. Just that one word, and he fell across one of the rocks. The rifle in his hands slipped free of his grip and clattered on the rocks before it struck the ground.

Lew gazed downward at the road, and there stood the girl, her rifle still pressed to her shoulder, a wisp of smoke spiraling from the barrel.

"Did I get him?" she said.

"You got him."

She pulled the rifle away from her shoulder and started walking back toward the place he had left her, as if she had no interest. As Lew scrambled forward, levering another cartridge into the chamber, he heard the horses clopping up the road. Their hoofbeats were muffled in the still, oppressive, cloud-laden air.

He bent over the man he had shot, turned him over. He was dead, a bullet hole in his chest just above his heart.

"They left their horses down here by the side of the road," Marylynn said. "I'll fetch 'em. We can sell 'em in Taos."

Lew did not reply. Marylynn was practical, if nothing else. She was also a pretty good shot, he thought.

The man she had shot was dead, too, a hole in the side of his neck. He hadn't bled much, because his heart had stopped pumping soon after he had struck the ground.

There was a folded piece of his paper in the man's pocket. Curious, Lew slipped it free, opened it up, and in the dim light began to read.

Fritz, you and Billy meet up with us in Santa Fe at the Tecolote Cantina. Wait for us.

The note was signed by Wayne Smith.

Lew's heart dropped a foot.

He folded the paper back up and stuck it in his pocket.

"What did you find?" Marylynn called up to him. He stood up.

"Nothing," he said.

"Get their guns. We can sell those, too."

"Yes, ma'am," he said, a sarcastic twang to his voice.

He stripped the men of their pistols and gunbelts, picked up their rifles, and walked down to the road. The clouds were even thicker now, lower in the approach to the pass. There wasn't a trace of sun and he shivered in the chill.

He slid the rifles into their scabbards and rolled up the gunbelts and shoved them in two saddlebags while Marylynn looked on, a faint smile on her face.

"Maybe the money will make up for some of the goods they stole from me and my father," she said.

"Ever kill a man before, Marylynn?" Lew asked, taking the reins of his horse from her hand.

She shook her head.

"No, never did."

"You seem pretty cool about it."

"I was mad," she said. "About what they did to my father. And I didn't want you to get killed, either."

"That might be quite a heavy load for a gal to carry. Killing a man like that. How old are you, anyway?"

"I'm nineteen," she said.

"And your father taught you to shoot like that?"

"Yes."

"You don't feel bad about killing a man?"

She shook her head again.

"Not about that man. He killed my father in cold blood."

"I would have gotten him. I was just about to squeeze the trigger when you fired your rifle."

"I couldn't see you. I just saw that man."

"And you don't have buck fever over it?"

"I might later. Not now. I'm just glad he's dead. I'm glad they're both dead."

Lew shivered, and it was not from the chill.

"I'll keep that in mind," he said.

"What do you mean by that?"

"I mean it's hard killing a man. Especially for a woman, I would think."

"You've killed a man before," she said. It was not a question.

"I reckon."

"And how did you feel?"

"I was plumb sick," he said. "And I still get the shakes afterward. Inside. As if I've done something wrong."

"But they were trying to kill you, Lew."

"I know. That doesn't make it any easier. Call it conscience, I guess."

"Well, of course I have a conscience. I sure don't go around killing people."

"Thank God," he said under his breath.

"What did you say?" she asked.

"Nothing. Let's get up to that pass. Over it, if we can. It'll be dark soon and it may come a snowstorm."

"We'll have to find shelter," she said.

Almost too eagerly, he thought as he put the spurs to Ruben. They each pulled a horse, and the going was slow. The road steepened and the silence closed in around them with the clouds.

After a time, they could see only a few feet ahead and there was no way Lew could tell if they had reached the top of the pass or not. But he began to scout for a place to hole up until morning.

He knew one thing.

He would sleep with his pistol close at hand. For all he knew, Marylynn might do away with him so she would have another horse and saddle to sell, plus more weapons to lay on the trader's table.

It was a chilling thought, but it was there, and he slipped into his winter coat, hoping he was wrong about Marylynn and her propensity to kill.

7

THE CLIMB UP TO THE PASS WAS HARD, GETTING HARDER. LEW spotted a game trail as the clouds began to hem them in, dropping visibility down to just a few yards. He turned his horse to the right, looked back to see if Marylynn would follow.

"What are you doing?" she said.

"We've got to find shelter. I think it's going to snow."

"Feels like it," she said, and turned her horse.

Lew nodded and tapped Ruben in the flanks. The horse humped up and climbed the even steeper game trail. It wound through thick stands of pine, spruce, fir, and juniper, then leveled off at a point where Lew thought they might have a chance to get out of the wind and, if they built a shelter, keep most of the snow off them during the night.

"Here?" Marylynn asked.

"As good as any. There are dead trees for firewood, rocks to reflect heat, plenty of spruce boughs for a shelter."

"You know how to do all this?"

"I grew up in the woods."

They climbed down from their horses and tied them up while Lew broke out ropes from the dead men's saddles and started running one of them through the O rings on the bridles.

Marylynn did the same with the horse she was riding and Ruben, using another rope. Lew helped her wrap the rope around a pine trunk and tie it securely. Then he secured the other horses in a different place, sheltered enough by spruce and juniper to keep the wind from doing its worst.

He found a rocky outcropping and spread the bedrolls next to it, scraped out a place for a fire, and ringed it with loose stones. Then he took his knife and began to cut spruce bows.

"What can I do?" she asked.

"Go around to the pines and break off the dry branches below the boughs. An old hunter I met up in Leadville told me they call this 'squaw wood.' It'll help us start a fire. Then you can start gathering any dry wood on the ground. I'll do the same after I build us a small lean-to."

"It's getting cold," she said.

"See if you can find a coat on one of those horses and slip into it," he said.

When he saw her a few minutes later, he almost didn't recognize her. She had on a big sheepskin coat that was too large for her. He could not see her hands or wrists. He suppressed a laugh as he continued to strip boughs from a spruce.

He sliced off the limbs from several spruce trees until he had enough poles to lean against the rock wall. He saved the cuttings and spread those over the ground underneath, putting the bedrolls on top. Then he cut more boughs and wove them into the poles until he had a fairly tight surface. The boughs were springy, but the weaving made them stronger.

He helped Marylynn gather more firewood, then started the fire just outside the lean-to. He piled rocks on one side so that the heat would reflect and keep the inside of their shelter warm.

He felt a dab of moisture on his face and looked up from the fire. A few small flakes of snow drifted down from the mountains above them.

"There was grain in their saddlebags," Marylynn said. "I fed the horses some corn and oats."

"Good. You warm enough?"

"I feel the chill. I found some airtights, too—beans and peaches. One of the men had some jerky. I didn't look in your saddlebags."

"There's some hardtack in a flour sack, and some beef jerky. I could eat a horse, but I'll settle for some beans and jerky."

"There's water in their canteens, too," she said, and marched off to start bringing goods to set inside the lean-to.

Small snowflakes fluttered down from the clouds. None of them stuck to the ground at first. They were weak and wet by the time they reached earth, but the fire sputtered until Lew got it going strong. He opened the airtight and set the beans next to the flames. He munched on hardtack and dipped it into the can. Marylynn followed his lead as they sat together next to the rock wall. She looked up into the maw of the storm, saw the swirling flakes mingle with the sparks from the fire.

"It's really quite beautiful, isn't it?" she said.

Lew looked up.

"Beautiful and mysterious. Sparks going up, flakes coming down."

"Never to meet," she said, in a musing tone. "Or if they do, they destroy each other."

Lew nodded, struck by the simplicity and truth of her observation.

They finished eating and washed their food down with water from the canteens. Marylynn crawled into the lean-to and slipped into her bedroll, pulling the covers up around her neck.

"I'll check on the horses," Lew said, feeding the fire with small sticks of dead wood. "See if I can find a big log to put on here to last the night."

The horses were fine, if a bit restless, but he tested the ropes. They would not run off. His only worry was that a bear or a cougar might come their way and either kill or spook them. It could not be helped. He would have to trust to Providence, divine or otherwise. He scouted the surrounding terrain and found a big heavy deadfall and lugged it back to camp. He put one end of it into the fire, sending a shower of sparks skyward. He could move the log during the night as it shortened from the burning.

By then the snow was falling more heavily. The flakes were larger, almost the size of a quarter, and they were sticking to the moistened ground. There was a white blanket of snow all around them, and the spruce boughs began to freckle with flakes.

Marylynn had brought the rifles inside the lean-to, and had set one by her bedroll, the other by his. He lay down and pulled the light blanket over him. By then it was dark and he could not see if Marylynn was awake or asleep. He could just hear her breathing in the silence of the snowfall.

"I keep thinking of my poor daddy lying back there in the cold ground," she said, and the sound of her voice startled him.

"Such thoughts will do you no good, Marylynn."

"I know. But I can't help it."

"Best to think of the good times you had with your daddy."

"I will. I will dream about him."

"Better go to sleep then. The other thoughts will keep you awake. The bad thoughts."

"You are so wise for a young man."

Lew said nothing. He listened to the tink of snow on the spruce boughs, so soft and lulling. He hoped the struts would hold even if it snowed a great deal. Perhaps the warmth of the fire would keep most of it melting. He could feel the heat inside their shelter. It was not much, but it was better than nothing.

"You are, you know. You're not much older than me. You must have had an interesting life."

"Be quiet, Marylynn. I want to go to sleep."

"I can't sleep."

"Then let me, will you?"

"How can you sleep? Those men are out there, too, not even in the ground. The wolves will probably get at them."

"Worms are probably already at work."

"Oooh. What a horrible thought."

"Shhh."

"I wish I were back home," she said.

He knew she wasn't going to shut up. He turned over and away from her, wishing she would.

"You're not going to ask me where I'm from, are you, Lew?"

"No, I'm not. I don't care. I'm tired and I'm sleepy."

"We're from Kansas. My mother died years ago, and my pa raised me. We had a farm and it dried up on us. My daddy wanted to come west to Santa Fe. He met a man who told him it was a rich city and that a man could get on well there."

"That's a hell of a thing to go on, make you leave your home. Where you grew up. Like following a pipe dream."

"My daddy was something of a dreamer, I reckon."

If he let her talk on, her voice might lull him to sleep. It was that soft. And hypnotic. But she paused, as if waiting for him to comment. He decided not to.

"Where are you from, Lew?"

"Mmmmf."

"Huh?"

"Arkansas," he said, his voice sizzling with irritation.

"Like Kansas, only with an a-r in front of it."

He did not reply.

"I'll bet it's pretty there. Kansas isn't pretty. It's just flat and has no trees. Not many, anyway. I just love these trees, the trees here in the mountains. I love the mountains, too, don't you?"

He grunted and pulled the blanket over his head.

"Just outside Abilene," she said. "Maybe five, six mile."

Lew didn't make a sound.

"That's where our home was. We started out with a big wagon, sold it and a lot of things in St. Louis. Daddy bought that little cart in Denver. We stayed there for a time— through the winter. I worked in a dry goods store, Daddy did blacksmithing. He thought he might do that in Santa Fe. But all his tools were in that cart, and I'm not much good with a hammer. I don't know what I'll do in Santa Fe."

"You got kin there?"

"No. I just don't know where else to go. Except where my daddy was going."

Then her voice broke off and he heard her muffled sobs coming from under her blanket. He clenched his fists. He wanted to knock her in the head to shut her up. She had ruined his sleep and would probably stay up all night pining for her pa. He got up and put more wood on the fire, just to get away from her.

When he came back, she had moved her bedroll next to his. He stumbled over her, not knowing she had done that.

"What the hell . . ."

"Lew, I want to be close to you. I miss my daddy."

He resisted the impulse to tell her that at least her daddy was sleeping undisturbed.

"All right," he said, and lay down next to her.

She was quiet for a while and he thought that she might have gone to sleep.

No such luck.

"Lew?"

"Yes."

"Are you still awake?"

"Obviously," he said.

"Do you think my daddy's in Heaven?"

"I don't know where he is, Marylynn. Can't you sleep?"

"No. My mind is just racing with thoughts about him and about those men we killed. Do you think God will punish us for that?"

"I don't think God punishes anyone. I think people punish each other and themselves. That's all the punishment they'll get."

"In this life, maybe. But what about afterward?"

"I don't think God is bent on revenge. Not my God anyways."

"You believe in God?"

"If you look at this earth and at the sky, it's hard to believe there isn't a God—someone or something that made it all."

"You are wise," she said.

"And you're a damned blabbermouth, Marylynn. Now, for God's sake, go to sleep."

"For God's sake . . . ," she said in a dreamy voice. He

closed his eyes and heard her breathing. The snow was still falling, and the silence was blessed. And he was wide awake, wondering about the girl lying next to him. What Fate had brought them together? What would she do in Santa Fe? She had almost been raped by three bad men out on the trail. She'd be a sitting duck in a town like Santa Fe.

Well, he wasn't going to worry about her. Not now. He had his own concerns, Wayne Smith being foremost. Perhaps Blackhawk would catch Smith, put him in jail, hang him. He hoped so. Then Lew could go on with his life and stop being a damned vigilante.

He fell asleep, finally. Later, he woke up because Marylynn had snuggled next to him. Her body was warm and soft. Her arm lay across his chest, and one of her legs was over his. He could feel her warm breath in his ear. He turned over, away from her, but she clasped both arms around him and pulled him tight against her. He could feel her young breasts pushing into his back.

"Marylynn," he said.

"I want you, Lew," she breathed. "I want you real bad."

"It's not right. You'd hate me come morning."

"No. No, I wouldn't. You're a good man. And I'm a virgin."

He let out a breath in a deep sigh. She rubbed against him, kneading her breasts on his back. She scooched her hips into him until he was cupped inside her thighs. It was warm, and his imagination caught fire.

"You should stay that way," he husked. "You'll find a husband one day and he'll want you pure."

"Don't talk no more, Lew," she said softly. "Just love me. Please?"

He turned over, and she held him tight. He felt her lips on his. He began to melt inside, and there was no escaping her, or himself.

The snow continued to drift down, silent as falling feathers. The night claimed them, locked them in its dark and stormy keep until there was no such thing as time and nothing mattered except that they melded together like lost waifs and were consumed by their mutual hunger.

Later, the wind came up and howled through the trees.

But neither of them heard it, nor cared that it blew snow in on them and covered their blankets for a time while the fire sputtered and spit, but blazed on like some beacon in a dark wilderness.

8

THE SNOW STOPPED FALLING SHORTLY AFTER MIDNIGHT, AL-
though Lew didn't know what time it was. He got up to feed
more wood to the fire and stepped into deep darkness with
no white flakes fluttering down from the sky. The big log
was nearly half burned, and he shoved the burnt end in and
added more wood on top until the blaze was chest high.
Then he crawled back into his bedroll and snuggled next to
Marylynn for warmth.

She was up before dawn, putting water on to boil for coffee, which she dug out of Lew's saddlebags. She found two
tin cups in one of the dead men's bags. She used the empty
bean can to boil the water. Lew awoke to the aroma of
steaming coffee and stepped outside the lean-to in the eerie
light. The ground was white, but the snow was only a few
inches deep, and the wind had blown most of it off the flat
places. Lew could see the road below, and it was fairly clear.

The coffee warmed him and so did the fire. Marylynn
brushed her hair with her hands, clearing out the tangles,
smoothing her auburn locks until she looked less disheveled.
There was a glow to her face, too, and Lew didn't think it
was from the fire.

"Breakfast?" she said.

"No. Too cold. Maybe we can get over the pass and into some warmer weather. I can gnaw on hardtack and jerky in the saddle if I get hungry. You?"

"I'm a little hungry, but the coffee's taking it away."

They were back in their saddles within the hour and taking it slow down the slope, letting the horses find their way. Ruben slipped a couple of times, but recovered quickly, and Marylynn's horse followed Ruben's track without difficulty.

"Thank you, Lew," she said, as they headed toward the pass.

"For what?"

"For what you gave me last night. You are quite a man."

"Was it like you expected?" She had been a virgin, just like she said.

"Ummm, I never dreamed anything could be so good, so sweet."

"You better keep those thoughts to yourself," he said.

"Why? I'm proud of what I done."

He had thought of Seneca a time or two during the night, but he had never made love to her. He didn't know why she crept into his thoughts, but she did, and when Marylynn was in the throes of her passion, he thought of Seneca and how it might have been if they had made love.

"Just don't make a habit of doing it with every man you meet."

"I wouldn't, and you shouldn't say such things. You shouldn't even think such things."

"Well, it was good and sweet, but we're not married and probably never will be."

"You needn't be so blunt about it."

"I didn't mean to be."

"You weren't a virgin, were you?"

"I don't think men are called virgins."

"You know what I mean," she said.

"No, I've done it before, a time or two. But it didn't mean much to me."

"Did I?"

He didn't even have to think about it. "Yes," he said. "Now, let it be, Marylynn. Let it be."

She pouted for the next mile, but they spoke no more of what they had done. When the sun came up, he saw how pretty she was. The light in her hair was radiant and her cheeks glowed as if she had rouged them. She looked happy, but he knew she was sad about her father, and she kept looking back as if trying to hold on to his memory.

"You don't tell me much about yourself, Lew," she said, as they neared the top of the pass.

"No, I reckon not."

"Secrets?"

"Nothing to talk about."

"Why did you leave Arkansas? You've got to be homesick, all alone like you are."

He wondered how much he should tell her. He was proud of none of it. His past followed him like a cloud, and the cloud cast a shadow. He was always under that cloud, it seemed, no matter how much he tried to ride out into the sun.

"My parents were murdered," he said, finally. "By two boys I went to school with. On my birthday."

Marylynn gasped.

"My, Lew, that's terrible. How awful. No wonder. You must have bad memories."

"Like you'll have for yourself, I reckon."

"Yes, that's true. So, you just packed up and left your home."

"Something like that. The law wouldn't do anything about those boys. They were rich boys. They killed an eyewitness, too."

"Are you afraid of them? I mean, afraid they'll kill you, too? If you stayed there?"

"No. They're both dead."

"Hanged? I thought the law . . ."

"No, I killed them. Now the law is after me."

"You didn't just . . ."

"No, I didn't just shoot them, if that's what you mean. They tried to kill me. So did the sheriff in the little town near where I lived. I shot him, too."

"You took the law into your own hands."

As if she knew, he thought. That was the way with people. They jumped to conclusions. All too quick. They formed opinions and built up prejudices. Like the law back home.

"No, I didn't intend any of it. I defended myself. The law thinks I'm a kind of vigilante. But I'm not. If the law worked, I'd let it work. It didn't work for me."

"You're on the run, then."

"Sort of. I reckon. I can't go back home. There's a U.S. marshal tailing me. He'd take me back and I'd likely hang. The justice back there wants blood. My blood."

"You poor man. I just can't imagine . . ."

"No, you can't, Marylynn, so just let it go and leave me be. I'm not proud of what I did, but I did what I had to do. Where there is no law, maybe each man who's in the right is the law. That's what I ran into and I don't carry any guilt in my kit. I stood up for myself and those boys are dead and gone. They dug their own graves."

"All right. I won't say anything. I can see you're still very touchy about it. And I don't blame you."

They reached the summit of the pass. The ground was wet from melting snow and there was mud underfoot. The air was thin, but the sun was warm. In the distance, Lew saw a hawk float out over the sloping land that led down to the plain. It looked majestic with the sun burnishing its wings to a faint bronze. He heard its high-pitched cry and then saw it fold its wings and plummet toward the earth.

Four or five quail scurried across the road. Ruben perked his ears, but didn't shy. Streams of water trickled down the mountainside and the sun headed for its noon zenith. Lew called a halt to rest the horses, let them graze on the grass that grew on the hillsides.

"What will you do in Santa Fe, Marylynn?" he asked.

"I don't know. Take in laundry, maybe. I have some money. My daddy made me wear the belt under my dress. He said it would be safer there. I can get by. What about you? Will you look for work there?"

"No. I'm riding on. I'll only be there a couple of days."

"Do you know someone there?" she asked.

"Nope. Nary a soul."

"Then, why . . . ?"

She realized she was prying into his life again and clamped her mouth shut. Just as well, he thought. He couldn't tell her why he was going to Santa Fe. He just knew he couldn't stay in Pueblo after Carol's brutal murder and with her kids dead, too.

"Just going to rest up there, get the lay of the land. I met a sheepherder, and he told me about a town called Socorro. I might go there."

"To herd sheep?"

Lew laughed.

"No. Just curious, I guess. He said his brother was in some kind of trouble. Piqued my curiosity, I reckon."

"So you're just what my daddy called a drifter, I guess. Not that there's anything wrong with that. But you don't put down roots. You're like one of those tumbleweeds we saw coming out west."

He laughed again.

"I guess so. Can't stay too long in one place. That marshal is dogging my heels."

"I see," she said, and turned pensive. She got off, walked away to heed nature's call. When she returned, she was holding a small flower she had picked. She had her nose amid its petals, sniffing it.

Lew watched her walk to her horse. She looked like a little girl, not a woman grown. He felt a tug at his loins when he thought about lying with her the night before, but he drew in a deep breath and turned away. Such thoughts, he believed, could lead to trouble. She would go her way; he would go his. And that was that.

They rode into Las Vegas late at night. They were both tired. Marylynn had been falling asleep in the saddle, and he'd had to jar her awake several times to keep her from falling. The town was dark, except for a few lanterns burning in cantinas and a small, dreary-looking hotel.

"I'll find a stable and maybe get us a room at that hotel," he said.

"It doesn't look like any hotel I ever saw," she said.

It was made of adobe and had a sign out that read BEDS, 50 CENTS.

"It'll have to do, I reckon."

"Do we each get a room?"

"No, I'll pay for one room. Unless you want to sleep by yourself."

"I just want to sleep."

"That's fine."

They found a stable. Nobody was there, but they unsaddled the horses, put them in empty stalls, and dipped grain from a bin, which they poured into troughs. There was water in the stalls. Only a few horses were there, whickering in the dark, clumping against the wooden sides of their stalls. The smell was heady with hay and horse apples.

They walked to the hotel, carrying their rifles. Lew draped the gunbelts over his shoulders, along with his saddlebags.

The Mexican inside the hotel woke up behind a crude desk that appeared to have been made out of a door sitting on stone blocks.

"Two dollars," he said.

"Sign outside says fifty cents," Lew said.

"That is for the dormitory. You want that?"

"No, a room."

"One room?"

"Yes, one room."

"Where you come from?" the clerk asked.

"North," Lew said.

"It is a long way to Santa Fe. You will rest here a few days?"

"No. We put our horses in the stables. I suppose we can pay the man in the morning. There was nobody there."

"Yes, there will be someone there in the morning."

Lew gave him two dollars and signed the register. He put down "Mr. and Mrs. Jones," smiling as he wrote.

"Here is a key, Mr. Jones."

Marylynn's eyebrows arched as she looked at him.

"Thank you."

"In the back. Third door on the left," the clerk said.

Lew and Marylynn walked down the dark corridor and found the door. The key worked and they went in. Marylynn lit a lamp. The bed was old and the mattress lumpy, the coverlet drab and worn. There was a table, two chairs, and a religious statue on the chest of drawers. A painting of Jesus hung in a cheap frame on one wall. The window looked out onto an adobe building next door. They heard a cat yowl down the street. Moonlight lit dust motes that rose from the dirty rug on the floor.

"Ugly, isn't it?" Lew said.

"I could sleep on bare rock," she said, and he could hear the tiredness in her voice. She set down the rifles and sat on the edge of the bed, taking off her shoes.

There was a small divan against one wall.

"You can have the bed, Marylynn. I'll sleep over there."

He set down the saddlebags, pistols, and rifles.

"Don't be silly," she said. "You can sleep in the bed with me."

"You need the rest," he said, aware of the lameness in his tone.

"Who are you to tell me what I need? I want you next to me. This is a frightful place. Did you lock the door? What if robbers come busting in on us?"

He chuckled.

"All right. Pick your spot. I'll climb in next to you."

He sat on the divan and took off his boots. The tiredness seeped through him. When he walked to the bed and looked down, Marylynn was already asleep. He turned down the lamp wick, lifted the chimney, and snuffed out the flame, pitching the room into total darkness. He slipped his pistol under the pillow on his side of the bed, within easy reach.

The bed groaned when he lay down on it and he could hear music, guitars playing, a man singing some mournful Mexican song down the street. He listened to Marylynn breathing for a few minutes and found that he was worried about what would happen to her after he left her alone in

Santa Fe. It was a disturbing thought. He closed his eyes and the night closed in on him, locking him deep in sleep.

He dreamed of barbed wire ropes and lawmen wearing badges as big as pie plates. And somewhere at the bottom of his mind, he heard the singing and the plaintive chords of a guitar. The voice he heard was his mother's, and none of it made any sense to him.

9

LEW AWOKE TO A LOUD POUNDING ON HIS DOOR. HE REACHED under the pillow and grabbed his pistol, his senses suddenly sizzling as if they had been electrified. Marylynn sat up, her eyes wide with fright, her hands over her mouth to suppress a scream.

"Shh. Wait here," he said softly, then strode to the door. He cocked the Colt in his hand. "Who is it?"

"You got horses in the stable?"

"Yes. What of it?"

"Somebody's claiming they're stolen. Another man wants to buy a couple of 'em."

"Who are you?"

"Jasper Pettigrew. I'm the day clerk here. Better get up and talk to those men out here."

"Be right out," Lew said.

"What is it?" Marylynn asked.

"Trouble, maybe. Somebody must have recognized the brands on those outlaws' horses. You stay here. Sit tight, and keep one of those rifles across your lap. When I get back, I'll bring us some breakfast."

"When will you be back?"

Lew sat on the divan, pulling on his boots. He strapped on his gunbelt and spun the cylinder of his Colt. All six rounds were there. Some men kept the hammer down on an empty cylinder, but he did not. He wanted all six when it came to a shoot-out. He hammered back to half cock and strode to the door.

"Soon, I hope," he said, and tossed her the key. "Lock this behind me."

Then he was gone, striding down the corridor, his right hand floating near the butt of his pistol. The desk clerk looked up.

"You Pettigrew?" Lew said.

"Yes. You're Mr. Jones."

Lew had to think for a minute. He nodded.

"Them two men over yonder by the front door. One wants to buy some horses, t'other'n says you better have a bill of sale."

"I'll take care of it," Lew said, and strode up to the two men.

"You Jones?" one of the men asked in a belligerent tone.

"Yeah," Lew said, looking the man up and down. He was burly and grizzled, with two days' worth of wiry bristle on his florid face. His corpulent neck pushed his collar tight. He had a scar across his jawline that was a livid white. The other man was short, thin, with a pencil moustache. He wore a battered Stetson and his hands were calloused, his skin the color of burnt cedar, as if he had been out in the wind and the sun every day of his life. "Who are you?"

The thin man nodded to the other.

"I'm Grimes," the heavy man said. "Charley Grimes, and I saw three of them horses you brung in last night. They're wearin' Circle C brands. Them horses belonged to friends of mine. Friends I been expectin' to ride down here from Pueblo."

"And you?" Lew asked the thin man.

"My name is Hiram Fogarty and I'm in need of a couple of horses. Benny Rodriguez, at the stables, told me you and a lady rode in last night and had yourselves four horses. So I thought if you didn't need all of 'em, I'd pay top dollar for the extry two."

"Meet me at the stables, Mr. Fogarty. I'll take this up with you there. Charley, let's go someplace where we can talk."

Fogarty left the hotel. Grimes stood there, glaring at Lew.

"We can talk right here, mister. I want to know about them Circle C horses you brung in."

"Outside," Lew said. "I don't want everyone to know my business."

Grimes stepped outside. Lew followed him. They both watched Fogarty walking toward the stables. People were out in the street, in front of stores, sweeping the dirt to make it smooth. A dog lazed in front of a building and a Mexican, wearing a large sombrero, squatted on a wooden pallet, fast asleep in front of a cantina.

Lew reached into his pocket and pulled out the folded piece of paper still there. He handed it to Grimes.

"You know Wayne?" Grimes asked.

"I do. I'm meeting up with him in Santa Fe, like the note says."

"Well, why didn't you say so? Me, too. But what are you doing with them horses?"

Lew hoped he could remember the names of the three men who had attacked Marylynn and her father. And he hoped his story was good enough to get by this belligerent man.

"Cal Weems, Billy, and Fritz got some good horses, asked me to take these on to Santa Fe, or to sell 'em and give them the cash when they got to the Tecolote."

"Don't sound right to me."

"Well, they didn't buy the new horses, Grimes."

Grimes stepped back, then smiled.

"You mean, they . . . ?"

"Stole 'em. Yep, that's what they did. So they had to hightail it, hide out for a few days."

"Well, they should have been here by now."

"Why don't you ride on to Santa Fe and meet up with all of us there?"

"You know Wayne's countin' on us all bein' there. He's got a pretty big job lined up for us."

"I know," Lew lied. "After he gets through in Denver, he'll be along."

"So you know about the Denver job."

"Sure," Lew said.

"I'm wonderin' why I never heard of you, or met you before. You from around here?"

"Missouri. I know Wayne from back in Bolivar."

"Oh, yeah, sure. Well, I reckon I'll just go on then, long as Fritz and Cal don't expect me to meet them and Billy here in Las Vegas."

"I don't think they do, Grimes."

Grimes still had the paper in his hand. Lew reached over and slipped it from his grasp. He folded it, put it back in his pocket.

"See you in Santa Fe, then, Mr. . . . ah, what did you say your name was again?"

"Ed Jones."

"Call you Ed. Be seein' ya."

"Yes. In Santa Fe."

Lew breathed a sigh of relief as Grimes walked across the street to a saddled horse. He waved as he rode off, and Lew waited until he was gone before he started toward the stables. But something about the man's good-bye wave and the slow pace of his horse put Lew on his guard. He had the itchy feeling that Grimes might not be leaving town right away. While he may have allayed the man's suspicions right off, Grimes might worry that bone some until he gnawed down far enough to become suspicious all over again.

Lew walked to the stables at a brisk pace. Las Vegas might be a dangerous place to linger for long, and there was a cash buyer waiting for him. If he could close the deal on those two outlaws' horses, that would be a little more money for Marylynn, to tide her over in Santa Fe until she found gainful employment.

Hiram Fogarty was inside the stables with Benny Rodriguez, looking over the horses Lew and Marylynn had brought in the night before. Hiram introduced Lew as "Mr. Jones."

"Call me Ed," Lew said to Benny.

"Good horses," Rodriguez said. "Did you see Mr. Grimes?"

"Yes. He headed on to Santa Fe, far as I know. I'll meet up with him there."

"So, you are not a horse thief," Rodriguez said, blunt as a hammerhead.

Lew shook his head and smiled.

"Nope."

"That Grimes, he was mighty suspicious."

"Well, that's his face card, I reckon. It doesn't hurt to have a little suspicion now and then. But I held the high hole card."

Rodriguez laughed. Lew thought the laugh might be a little forced. He didn't trust the man. For one thing, he had a big mouth. For another, he knew Grimes, and more than casually, it seemed.

"What do I owe you, Benny, for the board and feed? The missus and I are heading out after I take her some breakfast."

"Four dollars, Mr. Jones. But I will wait until you and Hiram complete your business."

Rodriguez walked away to let the two men talk, but Lew noticed that he busied himself well within earshot. He figured he could trust Benny about as far as he could toss a loop on a two-foot rope.

"Which ones was you wantin' to sell, Ed?" Fogarty asked.

"Those two geldings in the last two stalls. What's your offer, Hiram?"

"Fifty each."

"A hundred and I throw in saddles, bridles, blankets, and saddlebags."

Fogarty lifted his crumpled hat from his head, scratching it with fingers on the same hand.

"Well, I don't know."

"Take it or leave it. I figure we can get more for them in Santa Fe. And the longer I have to stand here, the higher the price goes."

"You got a deal, I reckon."

"Cash on the barrelhead."

"Why, sure. It's a little more than I wanted to pay, but I do need those horses. This country is awful hard on horseflesh."

"It's not too easy on human, either, Hiram."

Hiram laughed and dug into his pocket. He pulled out a wad of greenbacks and began to count them out in twenties. He counted them again, then handed them to Lew. Lew didn't count them, but slid the money into his pocket.

"I'll show you the saddles, blankets, and bridles," Lew said. "They're over there by the tack room. It was locked when we came in last night."

The two walked over. Lew sorted out the blankets and bridles, and moved two saddles over. He emptied two saddlebags and handed them to Fogarty.

"There you go, Hiram. Make sure you take those two horses in the end stalls."

"I will."

Rodriguez walked over.

"You want me to saddle them for you, Hiram?"

"You saddle one, I'll saddle the other."

Lew fished in his pocket, slid out a bill. He showed it to Rodriguez.

"You have change for a twenty?" he asked.

Rodriguez shook his head.

Lew put the bill back in his pocket and reached for his wallet. He opened it, pulled out four one-dollar bills, handed them to the stablemaster.

"Thanks, Benny," he said.

"Thank you, Mr. Jones."

The way he said "Jones" made the hairs prickle on the back of Lew's neck, but he didn't say anything.

"I'll be back in a while to get our horses," Lew said. "Thank you, Hiram. Good luck."

"Good luck to you, Ed."

Lew could see that neither man bought "Ed Jones" as his name. But in such country, a man could wear any name he chose, like a hat or a pair of boots. Maybe Jones was a little too common in these parts, he thought.

Lew found a café that was open and ordered two plates of huevos rancheros, *salciche*, and frijoles. The Mexican lady wrapped the food in dried corn husks and gave him a couple of paper napkins and a handful of fried tortilla chips to use as spoons. He paid and thanked her, then headed back to the hotel. The aroma from the food made his stomach growl with hunger.

Marylynn was dressed when she opened the door to his knock. She smelled the food right away.

"Oh, what did you bring me?"

"Us," Lew said. "Dig in."

They sat at the table and Marylynn unwrapped the food. It was still warm. Lew noticed that the woman at the café had put a couple of chili peppers in with the beans. He picked up two, offered one to Marylynn.

She shook her head.

"I ate one of those in Pueblo," she said. "I thought I was going to die."

"They ward off evil spirits, I hear," he said, biting the tip off one of the peppers.

Marylynn laughed.

Then, she laughed again when she saw Lew's eyes water and his mouth open to gulp in air.

"That is a hot little sucker," he gasped, clawing the table in mock pain.

"The little ones are the worst, I hear," she said.

"Now I know why the Mexicans drink tequila," he said. "It's to put out the fire from the chili peppers."

They ate and then Lew gave her the two hundred dollars in his pocket.

"Where'd you get this?" she asked. "Or is this your own money you're giving me?"

"Sold two of those horses we brought in. A hundred apiece."

Her eyes widened. "Well, you should get half."

"No, Marylynn. You'll need that money to start a new life for yourself in Santa Fe."

A sad look came over her face.

"You're just going to run off and leave me after we get there, aren't you?"

"No, I'll be around. For a while."

"For a while. I don't think I could bear to say good-bye to you, Lew. After what we've been through."

"Let's not cross that bridge just yet, Marylynn. Take the money. Let's go get our horses and leave this town."

"Did you have trouble this morning? You make it sound like we *have* to leave."

"Ah, it's not a real good town, Marylynn."

"You did have trouble."

"No, no trouble. Just, well, I just get a funny feeling now and then, you know?"

"No, I don't know. But let's go. I can see you're restless."

She put the money in her money belt, and he admired her legs when she lifted her dress. She caught him looking and smiled.

"Maybe there is a way to keep you close at hand, Lew," she said.

"I'm only human," he said, a sheepish look on his face.

Rodriguez was not in the stables when they returned and saddled their horses. Lew dipped some extra grain and filled one saddlebag for each horse. He crammed the stuff from the outlaws' bags in both his and Marylynn's until they were bulging.

They rode south out of Las Vegas, the sun casting their shadows to the west. The road was littered with wagon, horse, and cattle tracks, and he hoped one of the tracks belonged to Grimes.

As they rode, he looked over his shoulder more than once, and he scanned the land ahead for any movement—anything out of the ordinary. He had a hunch they might run into Grimes again, maybe in Santa Fe, maybe sooner.

And they still had a long way to go. And no guarantee of safety when they arrived.

Marylynn looked more beautiful than she had the day before, and he wondered if she was getting under his skin, like a mite working its way clear to his heart.

10

MARYLYNN HAD BEEN SILENT EVER SINCE SHE AND LEW HAD left Las Vegas, but Lew knew something was eating at her. She was fidgety, nervous. She kept slapping the tips of her reins across her left and right legs. First one, then the other. He was too busy scouting the terrain ahead and watching their backtrail to ask her what was on her mind. He knew that sooner or later she would tell him. Then he could deal with it, perhaps.

They had crossed the Pecos and headed west toward Santa Fe before she said more than two words to him. She had said nothing much at night camp, nor when they had had their coffee and nibbled on sweet rolls he had bought in Las Vegas, rolls that were turning hard in the heat and were like biting into iron by the second day.

"Lew, do you think much about that night?" she said. The morning sun was at their backs, and there was a glorious glow to the land ahead. Quail piped from atop the blooming yucca, and Joshua trees dotted the flat rocky ground. Doves whistled past them, twisting in the air like gray darts, winging their way to water.

"What night is that?"

"You know. That night. When I lost my virginity."

"Yes," he said. "I've thought about it some."

"What do you think of me?"

"Marylynn, I think you're a fine woman. A beautiful woman. I'm sorry you lost your virginity, if it bothers you, but it's not like a badge of honor you wear on your chest. It's just part of life, I reckon."

"I just wonder why I did such a thing. I wasn't brought up that way."

"You enjoyed it, didn't you?"

"Yes, very much. But I still don't know why I let myself be so . . . so loose."

He reined up Ruben and she stopped beside him. He could see that this had been worrying her ever since it had happened, and he had his own ideas about why she had given herself to him so freely.

"What?" she said. "Why are we stopping? Did I say something wrong?"

There was a flare of alarm in her wide eyes, and the expression on her face was one of genuine bewilderment.

"No, nothing's wrong. But you asked a good question. And I have an idea that I might be able to give you an answer. If it's that important to you."

"I guess it is, Lew."

"Okay. Do you know the story of Lot's wife, in the Bible?"

"Yes."

"What happened to her?"

"Yes. She looked back at Sodom and Gomorrah and was changed into a pillar of salt."

"What about afterward, when Lot and his daughters fled to the hills?"

"I don't remember what happened after that, I guess."

"Let's ride, and I'll tell you about it."

They clucked to their horses and headed toward Santa Fe. Lew kept talking.

"The daughters thought that everyone in the world was dead," he said. "So they conspired with each other to continue the human race."

"How?" Marylynn asked.

"They would bed with their father and have his babies."

Marylynn gasped. "Why, that's terrible," she said. "What an awful thing to do. Or even to think it."

"Remember, they thought they were the last humans on earth. They didn't want their race to die out."

"They surely didn't . . . not with their own father."

"Oh, yes, they did. They gave their father wine, and when he was drunk enough, they made love with him. They both took his seed inside of them and got pregnant." Lew paused. "In a way, that was what you were doing the other night."

"What? Not me."

Lew chuckled. "I know it's going to sound strange, Marylynn. But think about it—what happened that day. Your father was killed. You were left all alone, an orphan. For you, everyone in the world was dead. There was only me. So you turned to me so that you could carry on, like Lot's daughters, and repopulate your world."

"I never thought such a thing."

"No, you didn't think that way, but it was a natural human reaction. Your father was gone. There was no one else around but me, so you turned to me for comfort, for love. That's all that it was, and you should not feel bad about it."

"Is that what you think, Lew? That I gave myself to you because I was lonely?"

"If you weren't lonely, then you sure have a cold heart, Marylynn."

"I'm going to think about this. It's such a shock to hear. I mean, I do have sensibilities."

"Sure you do. That's why you did what you did. It wasn't bad. It was good. For both of us."

She looked at him, as if seeing him for the first time. "I wasn't wrong about you, Lew," she said after a few moments of reflection.

"No?"

"No. You are very wise for your years."

She said no more for a long while as they rode on through midday and the afternoon, passing wagons and carts, meeting others, waving politely and voicing perfunctory greetings. But they were strangers once again, each bearing their own thoughts, worrying them through their minds as a dog will gnaw on old bones.

Long shadows painted the road behind them and their horses. A dust devil danced a thousand yards away, swirling across the barren land like a dervish, hurling sand and dust in all directions. A jackrabbit bounced from hiding to escape and bounded into a clump of prickly pear, then froze until he turned nearly invisible.

"Lew," Marylynn said, "I've been thinking a lot about that night and the days and nights since then. Some of what you said kind of makes sense, in a way."

"I'm listening," he said, his gaze fixed on the dust devil, wondering if it would cross their path or come straight at them.

"You gave me something I longed for, something I wanted, but didn't know I wanted, or needed. Or maybe it was my father's death that gave me the gift. I—I don't know. I—I'm not real sure."

"Go on," he said.

She sighed and brushed away a strand of hair that dangled over her face. The sun made her hair shine as though it were spun from some gilded loom that left a russet sheen on every strand.

"You made me feel free," she said.

"Free? How do you mean?"

She sighed again, and her eyes shone with a fervent light as if she had tasted some exotic wine.

"I shouldn't say this, I know, but my father made me feel like a prisoner, ever since my mother died. I felt trapped, strapped down, sometimes strangled or suffocated by his love, his devotion. When I became a woman, Daddy kept an even more watchful eye on me. And every night, almost, he filled my head with dire warnings. Oh, I know he meant well, and all, but I was suffocating. I was a prisoner."

"So, when he died . . ."

"When he died, tragic as it is, I felt a kind of relief. Not right then, of course, but after . . . after you and I . . ."

"I think I know what you mean, Marylynn."

"Do you? When I say the words, they sound so heartless

and cold. I loved my father. I love him still. And I miss him. But . . ."

"But you feel free," Lew said.

"Yes," she said, the sibilant hissing with the force of her passion. "It is a sweet taste," she said fervently. "It tastes like honey and grape wine, this freedom you gave me, Lew. For the first time in my life, I am breathing free air. I could just shout with joy."

"Well, there's not a soul around. If you feel like yelling, Marylynn, you go right ahead."

She laughed, and Lew laughed with her. He had seen such inner happiness before, when the preacher in Osage had taken young girls to the creek and baptized them. Some had screeched, some had screamed, some had shouted out loud when they emerged, dripping wet, from the creek. He had once thought they screamed so because the water was so cold, but as he grew to maturity, he knew that they had been afflicted with a religious zeal that defied explanation. Marylynn's face now shone with that same expression he had seen on the faces of the young that the Baptist preacher had dunked in the creek back home.

The sun bronzed the clouds, and Lew turned off the trail, heading for the low hills to the north.

"Where are we going?" Marylynn asked.

"Make camp before it gets dark. I'm tired and I'm hungry."

"Me, too," she said.

The clouds turned golden, then reddened, finally paling to a salmon with tinges of red, and began turning to ash by the time Lew and Marylynn had gathered dry wood for a fire and laid out their bedrolls. The road to Santa Fe was not visible from the spot Lew had picked for their camp. They were behind a low ridge atop a hill, and if he stood on tiptoe, he could see the road.

"We'll maybe warm up some beans and cook some strips off that chunk of beef we brought," he said, "and then put out the fire before it gets full dark."

"Can't we keep it for warmth tonight? It got real cold last night."

"No, it's too bright an invitation."

"What do you mean?"

He shrugged. "Might be we don't want anyone to know where we are."

"I don't know anybody in these parts, Lew. Do you?"

"No, I reckon not. But you never know who might ride up in the night."

"Are you expecting someone to ride up to our camp?"

"Nope. It's the unexpected someone I'm worried about."

She cut the meat and boiled water for coffee, heated the pinto beans from an airtight.

"You act very strange, sometimes," she said. "Almost like a criminal."

"In the eyes of the law," he said, "I am a criminal."

"But you're not really."

She looked at him as he kicked sand on the fire, putting it out.

"Are you?"

He did not have a ready answer for her. There was a price on his head. But he had grown up to believe that a man was held to be innocent until proven guilty in a court of law. He had not been arrested, and he had not been charged with a crime. Yet, with a bounty on him, many people would think him guilty of some crime.

"I don't know, Marylynn. I'm a wanted man. That's enough for some folks."

"Well, not for me, it isn't. You're no more a criminal than I am."

"Eat," he said, squatting after one more look down the road. It was empty. They hadn't seen another traveler for at least two hours.

She sat and began eating. Every once in a while she looked over at him. He ignored her. She was starting to get under his skin, but he didn't know why. She just wouldn't let things be. She wanted to know everything and dig around in him until she found something she was looking for—whatever that was.

He was impatient to get to Santa Fe and leave her to fend for herself. She was the kind of woman who would throw a rope on a man and brand him the first time he dropped his guard. Well, that wasn't going to happen to him. Not with Marylynn. He had his own path to follow, and she had hers.

They slept a few feet apart. Marylynn fell asleep shortly after she pulled the blanket of her bedroll over her. Lew looked up at the dark sky, with its millions and millions of bright winking stars. Coyotes started singing before he fell asleep, a melodious chorus that seemed to sound from one place, then another. It was a beautiful sound, but he knew that it meant they were hunting something and that when they stopped singing, something had died—a rabbit, a bird, a deer, an armadillo, or a mouse.

Bright streamers of song, the high melodious yips and calls of the coyotes floated on the air, and he felt the wildness in the music, the savagery of the hunting canines. And there was something about it all that made him homesick, homesick for the Ozark hills and the deer that were moseying up from Osage Creek to feed all night in the hardwoods, nibbling on acorns and walnuts and hickory nuts. The coyotes would be bellowing like hounds back home, too, he knew.

He had listened to their night songs many times over the years and felt the same thrill he felt now, under the stars, so small a man in the immensity of the land and the sky, far from any human settlement, far from the law's long reach and the blindfolded lady holding a sword in one hand and scales in the other.

He felt free, but was he, really?

Lew fell asleep, not knowing the answer to that question.

Was any man ever truly free?

The question took him deep down into the ocean of sleep as the silent stars looked on and the moon spread its pale pewter light across the desolate and vacant land.

11

THEY DROPPED DOWN OUT OF THE PINES, HAVING PASSED THROUGH a mountainous stretch that brought them a welcome coolness that last afternoon. The sign outside the town, its letters faded from wind and weather, proclaimed it to be Glorieta. It was a small town of adobe dwellings, a *tienda*, a livery stable, blacksmith's shop, and a small café that reeked of corn tortillas, chorizo, and frijoles *refritos*. Marylynn was hungry and wanted to stop. There were some hitch rings buried in the earth outside the café, and they tied their horses to these and walked inside through the open door, where flies buzzed and moths clung to the jamb like tiny mauve bats.

There was only one other patron inside, sitting at a small counter with a cup in front of him, no saucer, and a pint of tequila next to it. He was talking to a woman behind the counter, a matronly, moon-faced lady with neatly coifed hair streaked with gray. They were speaking Spanish and didn't seem to mind that they could be overheard.

"Pepe," she said, "you must be careful with men like that. You should not cheat such men. He is a bandit, I know that. A killer."

"Charley did not care. I have cheated him before." Pepe had short-cropped hair, black with flour-white sprigs salted in his sideburns, and a moustache waxed to a high black sheen. He was muscular from the waist up, his hands gnarled and scarred from years of manual labor at the blacksmith's forge.

They both laughed.

"I do not like the way he looks at me, Pepe. He takes my clothing off with his eyes."

"That is why I made him pay me the five dollars in silver for fixing the shoe of his horse. Charley wanted to give you his sausage, Lupita, and you would have made him pay even more for the privilege of lifting your dress."

Lupita's face reddened and she glanced at the two gringos who slid chairs out from a table near the door.

"Pepe, you go back to the stables. I do not lift my skirts for such trash as Charley Grimes, that son of bad milk, that white bastard."

"Oh, you have customers, Lupita. We will talk about lifting your dress tonight when I have finished my work."

"We will talk about that five dollars you have in your pants, Pepe, before there will be any talk of my dress."

Pepe rose and stretched his arms out to Lupita, but she backed away and cocked a thumb toward the doorway.

"Go now," she said, "and do not drink too much this afternoon."

She picked up a slate tablet from below the counter and walked to the table, setting it down in front of Lew. The tablet clacked, and some of the chalk flew off the letters. The bill of fare was in Spanish.

"Can you read that, Lew?" Marylynn asked. "All I can smell is beans, and I've had enough of those."

"I can read it. You want steak?"

"Umm, yes."

As Pepe left, he pinched Lupita's behind and she swatted at him, fanning the air with her hand but smiling at him as he stepped through the doorway.

"Dos bistecas, senorita, y dos botellas de cerveza, por favor."

"Oh, you speak the tongue," Lupita said in Spanish. "The beer is not cold, but it has coolness. Do you wish to have beans with your beefsteak?"

"Do you have potatoes or squash?" Lew said, also in Spanish.

"We have potatoes. They will cost fifty cents over the price of beefsteak and beans."

"She will have the potatoes, and I will have the beans with my beefsteak," Lew said.

"I will tell the cook," Lupita said.

Lew glanced beyond her at the wall between the counter and the front door. There was a large corkboard there, and pinned to it was a flyer with his name on it and a drawing of his face that had resembled him nearly two years before. He saw the word REWARD in large block letters and under that, an amount: $1000. Beneath that, he read the words Dead or Alive.

"A moment, senorita," Lew said to Lupita as she turned to go.

"Yes? What is that you wish?"

"I heard you talking with your friend. Was Charley Grimes here this day?"

"You are a friend of Charley Grimes?"

"I know him."

"He was here. Very early. His horse threw a shoe last night, and Pepe made him a new one. Charley ate his breakfast here and then he left. He said that he was going to Santa Fe. But he is always coming and going."

"Yes. Did he look at that flyer over there on the wall?" Lew asked, pointing to it.

"He looked at it for some minutes, yes, and he asked me for one. I have some more if you would like one. You can get it when you leave."

"Thank you."

Lupita did not look at the flyer, but headed for the kitchen. There was an opening behind the counter and she disappeared through it. Lew could hear her giving his order to the cook. He strained to see if she said anything about him or Charley Grimes, but she did not. She talked to the cook about Pepe and his five dollars.

Marylynn leaned over the table and whispered to Lew. "Is that you on that poster?"

"Are you wanting to claim the reward?" he said, and then instantly regretted his coarse remark.

"No, of course not. It doesn't look like you."

"It's the four-day beard."

"Do you think that woman recognized you?"

"People never look at Wanted flyers. The only ones who do are lawmen and bounty hunters."

"Who is this Charley Grimes?" she asked.

"He was one of the men waiting to see me at the hotel in Las Vegas. I think he's an outlaw. I made him think I was one, too."

"Lew, you must be careful," she said. "That's an awful lot of money."

"Do you want coffee with your breakfast?" he said, hoping to change the subject. Grimes was on his mind, but he didn't want him ruining his meal.

Marylynn shook her head.

"No, just water," she said.

When Lupita returned with their breakfast on a tray, Lew ordered two glasses of water.

"Ten cents a glass," Lupita said. "We do not have much water here sometimes."

"That's all right."

Lupita set the plates before them and then went to draw water. She returned with two glasses as Lew and Marylynn cut their steaks.

"Thank you for the potatoes," she said. "They're a little raw, but a welcome change from beans."

"They're a mite quieter in the stomach, too," Lew said with a smile.

He heard whistling from the kitchen, a tune he did not know. A moment later, out of the corner of his eye, he saw the waitress walk to the counter, then a rustle of papers. She went back into the kitchen, carrying one of the flyers that had been on, or under, the counter. The whistling stopped.

"Better eat up, Marylynn," Lew said softly. "I think we might have to leave in a hurry."

She looked up from her plate, a surprised expression on her face.

"Why? What's wrong?"

"I think the waitress and the cook might be trying to make a little money."

Marylynn looked even more puzzled than before as she chewed on a piece of steak.

A moment later, the doorway to the kitchen filled and Lew saw a short, burly man come to the counter. He peered at Lew with squinting eyes, a rotund Mexican wearing a white apron stained with grease.

Lew nodded to him.

"That must be the cook," Marylynn said.

"How is the food?" the cook asked, with a crooked grin.

"Fine, fine," Lew said.

Then the cook walked around the counter. His hands were out of sight until he reached the opening to the dining area. When he came through it, Lew saw a large butcher knife in his hand. He waddled over to the table. Lew rose from his chair, his napkin dropping from his lap.

"Don't you move," the cook said, "or I cut you."

The cook swung the knife, slicing the air.

Lew didn't hesitate.

He waded toward the man, crouching low. As the cook lifted the knife to strike, Lew leaped at him and grabbed his wrist. They wrestled. The cook had a strong grip on the knife, and he tried to jab Lew in the neck. Lew squirmed out of his way and kicked the cook in the shin.

The cook grunted but didn't cry out. He wrested his arm from Lew's grip and circled, holding the knife out from his body, feinting, jabbing, looking for an opening. Lew circled with him, then paused.

The cook lunged at Lew.

Lupita cried out. *"Cuidado, Pedro."*

Lew backed up, and as Pedro thrust the knife at his belly, he grasped his wrist again and twisted. This time Pedro cried out in pain. But he still held on to the knife.

Marylynn slid her chair away from the table and stepped to a spot behind Lew.

"I kill you," Pedro said, and twisted hard, freeing his knife hand once again.

Lew kicked Pedro in the crotch, but the blow seemed to have no effect on the man. As Pedro backed up, his breath washed over Lew, assailed his nostrils with the dry musk of mescal or pulque. Lew saw that Pedro's eyes were glazed and the veins next to his nose stood out like buried red wires or thin worms.

Pedro swiped the air close to Lew's face, and Lew backpedaled to escape his rush. As Pedro passed close, Lew drove a fist into his side, his knuckles disappearing into soft flesh. The blow seemed to have no effect on Pedro.

Pedro whirled, swung around, brandishing the knife at a lower level. He charged Lew, aiming the knife straight at Lew's groin. Lew twisted out of his way and hammered another fist into Pedro's bulging neck. He felt the shock explode in his wrist and travel up his arm. As Pedro passed this time, Lew clubbed him with his left fist, smashing his nose. He heard a crack as a bone broke and blood gushed from Pedro's muzzle.

Pedro staggered, but regained his footing and came at Lew again, slashing up and down with his knife and straight across, driving Lew back against the counter. Lew slid sideways to escape the onslaught, and Pedro scratched a furrow in the counter.

Just then, Lupita reached down behind the counter and came up with a sawed-off shotgun in her hands. A double-barreled shotgun, the bluing nearly gone. She brought it up to her shoulder. That's when Marylynn stepped up to Lew and jerked his pistol free of its holster.

Lupita put her thumb on one of the shotgun's hammers, and Marylynn cocked the Colt and stuck it out, aimed straight at Lupita's face.

"You cock that shotgun, and I'll shoot you dead," Marylynn said. "Drop it on the counter and step back. I mean it."

Lupita struggled with the command. Her hand shook, and her thumb hardened over the hammer, rigid as bone.

"Now," Marylynn said, and moved closer.

The expression on Marylynn's face told Lupita all she needed to know. She set the shotgun down and backed away, holding both hands up in the air.

Pedro slashed downward and ripped into Lew's sleeve, slicing his arm with a shallow cut. Blood oozed from the wound. The sight of blood seemed to excite Pedro even more and he followed up with a wild swing at Lew, meant to decapitate him. Lew moved his head just in time, then grappled with Pedro, grabbing both arms right at the elbows and pushing with all his might to throw Pedro off balance and backward.

Lew felt the muscles, the strength in the man. And Pedro outweighed him by at least forty pounds. Sweat broke out on Lew's forehead, beaded up in the furrows, oozed from his hairline, streaked his face. Pedro hardly looked winded.

"Cabron," Pedro spat and whipped both arms upward, breaking Lew's grip.

Marylynn reached for the shotgun and lifted it off the counter. She continued to hold the pistol aimed at Lupita, who stood in the kitchen doorway, her eyes wild and flashing with fear and anger.

Marylynn held the shotgun in her left hand, the barrels pointed downward at the floor. She was as steady as a carpenter's level.

Pedro grunted and charged Lew, his nostrils flaring like a bull's, the veins on his neck pressing against the flesh, his skin sleek with the oil of his sweat.

Lew feinted, bobbing first one way, then the other. Pedro rushed him and Lew stepped to one side, drew his right arm back as if he were going to hurl a javelin, and drove his fist into Pedro's temple with such force that he felt the shock all the way to his shoulder. The blow staggered Pedro, and as he fought for balance, Lew stepped in closer and chopped downward into the muscle of Pedro's arm. Pedro's fingers opened slightly as an electric charge surged through his wrist. Lew grabbed for the knife and wrested it from the man's hand.

Then, as Pedro spun around, Lew drew back his right leg and kicked the cook square in the groin. Pedro doubled over in pain and went to his knees.

Lew turned, grabbed the shotgun from Marylynn's hand, and, taking it by the barrel, swung it in a wide arc. The stock slammed into Pedro's head with a resounding crunch, and they all heard the wood crack. Pedro's eyes rolled back in their sockets for a moment. He stuck out an arm like a drowning man grasping for a life ring, and then toppled over, unconscious.

Lew cracked open the breech of the shotgun and ejected the two shells. Then he threw the gun on the floor and turned to Lupita.

"You're lucky I didn't kill you both," Lew said to her. "Marylynn, hand me my pistol and then pack up our food. We'll eat on the way out of this town."

Marylynn sprang to the table with alacrity and began piling food into a cloth napkin.

"If anybody follows us out of town, lady," Lew said to Lupita, "I'll come back here and blow you and Pedro to kingdom come. *Me entiendes?*"

Lupita nodded, her eyes wide with fright.

Lew grabbed one of the flyers on the way out and tucked it inside his belt. In moments they were back in their saddles and riding west toward Santa Fe.

Lew kept looking back, but nobody followed them. A few minutes later, he guided them off the road and they followed the sun westward, well away from any would-be pursuers.

"You really are a wanted man, Lew," Marylynn said. "I was scared."

"Let me tell you something, Marylynn," he said. "If I ever get in another fight, I hope you're watching my back. You did just fine."

"That cook was trying to kill you," she said, as if dumbstruck.

"That's what a price on your head does to people," he said. "I'm just a way to make a few extra dollars for folks who ought to know better."

"Well, I wouldn't want to go up against you."

She reached out and touched his arm, saw the blood, the ripped sleeve. He held his arm up and looked at it himself.

"Can you sew?" he asked.

"There's a lot of things I can do, Lew. If only you'd let me."

He didn't answer, but reached for the bundle of food Marylynn had in her lap.

"I'm still hungry," he said. "But tonight, we'll eat in Santa Fe."

"Together?"

"Yes, together. I owe you for what you did back there. That fool waitress would have filled us both full of buckshot."

"I never thought of that," she said. "I just didn't want her holding a shotgun on you."

"You're a good woman, Marylynn," he said. "You'll go far."

She gave him an odd look, but Lew paid no attention. He took a piece of steak from the bundle and stuck it in his mouth, then handed the food back to Marylynn. She looked at it, and then her face drained of color and she grabbed her stomach.

Lew knew she was going to be sick.

12

THE SNOWY PEAKS OF THE SANGRE DE CRISTO RANGE GLIS-
tened in the late afternoon sun like an ermine mantle sprinkled with silver and golden dust. Santa Fe lay in view, a
sprawl of adobe buildings that glowed with an orange fire.
A thin pall of smoke hung over the town, and as Lew and
Marylynn rode in, they could feel the energy and vibrancy
of the inhabitants. Carts pulled by burros traversed the busy
streets, vendors displayed wares of blankets and pottery and
vestments and utensils, children raced to and fro playing
with sticks and balls, and women trundled babies from shop
to shop like travelers on an excursion to a foreign land.

"What a beautiful place," Marylynn exclaimed, her gaze
taking in the splendor of a city that seemed to rise magically
from the barren desert.

"It's quite a town, I hear," Lew said, and began looking
for a place to board their horses. He knew, from experience,
that there was probably a town plaza, and that this road, and
all others leading into Santa Fe, was arrowed straight toward
the center of the city.

None of the people on the street paid any attention to
them, and they saw others on horseback as they neared the
heart of the city. The sunset emblazoned the clouds with

shimmering patinas of gold, and rays shot out from some of them like some wondrous fountain that bespoke the majesty of nature and, perhaps, the glory of a supreme being. Marylynn gazed at the heavens like a wonderstruck child, while Lew looked closely at the cantinas and eateries that seemed to appear on nearly every block.

"Where are we going?" Marylynn asked.

"I'm going to find a stable and a hotel," he said. "Then we can look for a place to eat."

"Are we staying in the same room at this hotel?" she asked.

"Marylynn, you've got to get over your attachment to me. I'll be riding on, soon, and I'm riding alone. You'll have to find your own way."

"I don't know if I can," she said. "And you need someone to look after you, Lew. I've already seen what kind of trouble you can get into. And then, there's that flyer, following you wherever you go."

Lew pulled out the scrap of paper he had taken from the café and studied his likeness.

The drawing showed him clean-shaven, with short hair. He touched fingers to his beard and stroked the stubble as if coaxing it to grow.

"I'm going to let my beard and hair grow out," he said. "I doubt if anyone will recognize me. We're a long way from Arkansas."

"I feel like a castaway," she said, pouting.

"You mean a castoff."

"That, too."

He laughed.

"Marylynn, you have your own life to live. I have my own."

"But I want to be with you. Please." The pleading in her voice made him squirm inside his skin.

"I wouldn't know what to do with you, Marylynn. I'm not married. Never have been. I don't have a job. I couldn't support you. I couldn't even settle down. I'd always be looking over my shoulder. A wanted man."

"Maybe you should think about getting married. Settling down. You need someone to look after you, Lew. We've passed at least two livery stables. Didn't you see the signs?"

The truth was, Lew wasn't looking for the stables yet. He was looking for the Tecolote Cantina, and he saw it just when she asked the question. But he wasn't going to tell Marylynn what was on his mind.

"I guess I missed them," he said. "But I don't see any hotels."

"There were some up those two streets where the stables were," she said. "I declare, you must be a country boy."

He laughed.

"Yeah, I guess I am."

"Well, are we going to board our horses or just keep riding all night?"

"We can go back. You show me the sign."

They turned their horses. The sun was down behind the mountains, but the glow was still in the sky. Bats flapped overhead like harbingers of dusk, and the temperature began to drop. A few oil lamps glowed in store windows.

Marylynn pointed to a sign that read STABLES, 1 BLOCK. They turned down that street, which bore the name Caballo Street. There were two hotels in the first block and one in the next, across from the small livery and blacksmith's shop. All of the buildings were made of adobe brick. None were close together. There were cobblestones in front of the hotels and hitch rails as well as rings.

"That looks like a nice one," Marylynn said, pointing to the first hotel they passed. It was called El Nopal, and there were two large pots flanking the entrance, both filled with cactus plants.

"We'll see," Lew said.

The next hotel they passed was called The Majestic, and, like the first, it was two-storied, with a balcony on the second floor. It had no plants outside, but looked clean and inviting to a pair of tired riders.

The stable was at the end of the second block, across from a hotel called El Palacio. Its lobby was visible from the street, since it had plate glass windows and was well lighted with oil lamps that glowed invitingly onto the darkening street. The stable took up space for four hotels and was called Caballero Stables. A square of orange light stood outside the open doors of the first entrance, and there were hitch rails along the front of the entire complex.

They dismounted out front and wrapped their reins around one of the hitch rails and walked inside. The aroma of horse dung and hay assailed their nostrils. A horse whinnied at the far end and a man emerged from one of the stalls. He wore a straw hat, faded blue denims, and a blue chambray shirt. When he drew close, he spoke to them in English.

"You wish to board your wagon here?" he said. "I am Alonzo, the owner, at your service."

"Two tired horses," Lew said.

"Ah, you will stay the night—longer, perhaps?"

"Longer, maybe," Marylynn said, with a mite too much eagerness, Lew thought.

"At least one night," Lew said. "What do you charge for boarding?"

"You will stay at the hotel across the street? I own that, as well, and if you stay there, then it is only one dollar for each horse. If you do not, then the cost is two dollars for each horse."

"What does the hotel charge for the night?" Lew asked.

"One room or two?" Alonzo said. He was a short, muscular man, clean-shaven, with gnarled hands that had weathered many a rope burn. He had an affable smile and the whitest teeth Lew had ever seen.

"One room," Marylynn said, and Lew sighed.

"Yes, one room," he echoed.

"For you, because you are young and you are tired, the cost will be only two silver dollars for the night. If you stay a week, only twelve dollars. Is that too dear for you?"

"No," Lew said. "That will be fine."

"I will get your horses. You just walk across the street and tell the clerk at the desk that Alonzo said you are to have the special rate, for one night or for one week."

"Thank you," Marylynn said, beaming.

"Yes, thanks," Lew said, feeling as if she had a rope around his neck.

"You may pay the livery charge at the hotel," Alonzo said. "There is a room for dining and the food is very good. And we serve honest drinks at very reasonable prices."

"You speak very good English," Lew said. "Better than I speak Spanish."

"I had the education from the Catholic school," he said. "I went to college in Mexico City to learn the business, but I learned the English when I was very young."

Alonzo walked outside with them and waited until they had removed their rifles and saddlebags, then led their horses into the stables.

"Do not worry," he said. "I will take good care of your horses. My boy will be here soon and then I will take my supper at the hotel. Perhaps I will see you there later."

"Maybe," Lew said, taking Marylynn by the arm before she could get words out of her open mouth. He hustled her across the street toward the hotel.

"My, what a nice man," she said. "I like Santa Fe already."

Dangerous thinking, Lew thought. A young woman could be lulled into a sense of well-being so easily. Santa Fe was an old town, wise in the ways of the world. And like all such towns, its denizens were waiting to pounce on the unwary, the unsuspecting, the innocent. But he did not want to think of these things. After tonight, she would be on her own, out of his sight and out of his mind. He could warn her, but he would not go so far as to throw his lot in with hers, no matter how vulnerable she might be.

He paid at the desk for a room and the livery. One night only. Much to Marylynn's disappointment.

When she saw the room, Marylynn turned to him. "Oh, it's so nice here. Couldn't we stay for a week? Get to know the town? Do some exploring. At least until I can find some gainful employment."

"Marylynn, what you do is your own business. I'm staying for one night, that's all."

"Oh, you hardheaded stubborn old mule," she said. "You want to spoil everything."

"No, I don't, Marylynn. What's so special about this place? It has a bed, a table, two chairs, a chamber pot, a dresser, and a wardrobe. There are thousands of these rooms all over the West."

"But it was such a long tiring ride here, Lew. And as soon as we get here, you want to leave. You just can't wait to get rid of me, can you?"

"I'm not trying to get rid of you. I have my own life to live. And you have yours. This is a dead horse. Let's not beat it anymore."

She did everything but stomp her feet. He watched her wash up for supper and waited until she was ready to go down before he took to soap and water. She glared at him the whole time from the window, where she gazed out on the city, its adobe buildings softened by night, its lights full of bright orange promise, the snowcapped mountains shining under stars and a rising moon.

They ate in the dining room, at a small table that looked out on a veranda bathed in moonlight, with a fountain that glistened in the golden glow of lamplight.

"It's so romantic," she said. "I wonder why nobody is taking their meals outside on that lovely veranda."

"Probably because they'd be eaten alive by flies and mosquitoes," he said.

"Lew, don't you have any romance in you whatsoever?"

"Not that I know of," he said, chewing on a tender morsel of steak smothered in onions.

She huffed a little, but left him alone while she ate and admired the romantic view. He wished now that he had just dropped her off and gone to another hotel. She was as hard to get rid of as red chiggers in high grass. His only hope was that she would still be asleep in the morning when he up and left her.

When they were drinking their coffee after finishing their meal, she reached across the table and put her hand atop his.

"I am going to miss you, Lew. I wish I were going with you."

"I wish you well, Marylynn. Let's not say good-bye yet. I don't much like good-byes, anyway."

"I don't like them at all."

"Maybe you'll change your mind by morning and let me go with you," she said.

"No, I will not. And that's final."

She withdrew her hand and glared at him.

"I wish my father were here, alive," she pouted. "He'd take the strop to you and beat you to a fare-thee-well."

"You must have had a mean father."

"How dare you say a bad thing about my father."

"You said it. Not I."

"Lew, you are impossible."

"Let's keep it that way," he said, and turned away from her.

It was good to rest up in the city, to be at a destination. But looking out at the veranda and the stars, the moonlight, he knew he was more at home out there, bedroll on the ground, horse nibbling grass nearby, only the silent stars for company. He wondered if it would always be so.

Her cup clattered against her saucer as if she had jangled them deliberately to get his attention.

"I'm ready to return to the room," she said. "Unless you want to explore the town, see what sights it has."

"I do not. I'm tired, Marylynn."

"Well, I'm tired too, Lew. I'm ready to go to bed."

He studied her face. There was a ferocity about the woman that was almost admirable. But she could cling to a man like a wood tick and suck blood until she almost popped. In the lamplight, he had to admit, she was beautiful. Like a river at night, a river running deep. There was a mystery about her, the mystery of woman, perhaps, and a strength such as his mother had possessed. She was fascinating, even alluring. He knew he had to be on guard this night, more than all the others. She knew he was leaving her in the morning. He would put nothing past her in her desire to have him stay.

"Marylynn, before we go up, there's something I wanted to ask you. Just to satisfy my curiosity."

"Sure. Ask me anything."

"Back there in Glorieta, when you had my pistol trained on that woman, would you have shot her if she hadn't put down the shotgun?"

She looked at him for a long moment, her gaze direct, unwavering. Her eyes glowed with a sunken fire like the coals in a blacksmith's forge.

"What do you think?" she asked.

"I asked you," he said.

"She was going to shoot you, Lew. I've already killed one man who tried to do that. What makes you think I wouldn't have killed a woman trying to do the same thing?"

"That's what I wanted to know," he said, and scooted his chair away from the table. "I just hope you don't get into the habit," he said. "On anybody's account."

"Like you, you mean," she said, and her words stabbed him in the heart.

Hell, he thought, *hath no fury like a woman scorned.*

13

SHE WASHED THE DRIED BLOOD FROM HIS ARM WITH A WET cloth. The cut was not deep, and Lew knew it would not take long to heal. It didn't hurt, just stung a little in places.

"You should have some merbromin on it. Iodine, maybe."

"Neither of which we have here in the room," he said.

She leaned back in her chair and dropped the damp cloth onto the table. The room was on the first floor, at the back of the hotel. The view from the window was not much, a vacant lot overgrown with weeds that had caught scraps of paper, pieces of thin cloth, and tumbleweeds. Other buildings on either side loomed faint in the darkness.

"Lew," she said, "what was it like when your folks . . . when you lost your ma and pa?"

"You're thinking about your daddy," he said.

"Yes. You remind me of him, in a way."

"How so?"

"I don't know. Your quietness, maybe. But you're gentle. He was hard."

"Daddies have to be hard on little girls, maybe."

"Are you going to answer my question? Please. I want to know."

"My ma and pa were brutally murdered," he said. "It is not something I like to think about. They were killed on my birthday, so I have a permanent reminder of how they died."

"I don't mean those kinds of thoughts, Lew. I meant, afterward. When you were alone and they were gone. What did you think? How did you feel?"

"Probably like you feel, Marylynn. One minute they were alive, the next minute they were gone. There was an emptiness in the world. My pa . . . I miss him still. It's like there's a hole in my life, in all life."

"That's how I feel. I keep thinking he'll walk through that door there. He—sometimes, he feels right close to me. And at others, he seems so far away I can't even remember what he looks like."

"It's going to be that way for a long time, Marylynn. Maybe you never get over it. I don't know."

"What do you mean?"

"I dream about my father. And my mother. I can't make good sense of the dreams, but there is the feeling that he is still alive and still giving me good advice."

"That hasn't happened to me, yet," she said. "At least I don't think it has."

"Each person is different, I guess."

"What else?" she asked.

Lew could hear the screechy squeak of a windmill somewhere outside. It was a forlorn sound and reminded him of other times when he was alone and he heard things.

"Sometimes, when I'm alone in a room like this," he said, "I hear my father's footsteps outside the door, or somewhere in the building. I know it's him because of the rhythm and because I remember his gait, the way he walked. I know he's just outside, and I have the feeling that he's going to walk through the door and put his hand on my shoulder."

"Oooh, you're giving me the chilblains, Lew."

"Sometimes, I think he's in the same room. That walk of his, and it's as if I can hear him breathing like when he would come in to my room at night after I'd gone to bed and he wanted to see if I was asleep or say good night. It's a genuine feeling. I know he's there. Maybe his spirit, I don't know. But he isn't. He isn't there. And he never will be."

"That's so sad, Lew."

He got up from the table as if to shake off the emotions that gripped him.

"I'm going to bed, Marylynn. I want to get an early start."

He yawned and stretched his arms.

"I hope tomorrow never comes," she said, in a dreamy voice.

"It will."

"I don't know what I'll do without you. No one to talk to. No one to see after me . . ."

"You'll do fine. I have some advice for you, though. If you'll take it."

He turned from the window and looked at her. There was an eagerness in her expression that made him think of a dog wagging its tail, begging for any scrap of attention.

"Yes, I will," she said.

"Sell that big Colt .45 and get yourself a smaller weapon, a pistol that feels light in your hand. A Smith & Wesson .38, maybe, or a Lady Colt, a .32 caliber. That gun's too big for you. And wear dresses that don't get in your way when you have to run from trouble or draw that pistol from your purse."

"Do you think I'm going to be like you?" she asked.

"Like me?"

"Always on the run. Always facing someone who wants to kill you."

"No, I don't think that."

"You sound like you do."

"I'm tired. I'm going to sleep."

"I'll sit up awhile. I want to think about tomorrow. And the day after."

He didn't remember her coming to bed, but sometime during the night, he felt her arm across his chest, and then she was stroking the side of his body with the other hand. He felt her unbuttoning his trousers, and he didn't stop her. He heard the rustle of her clothes as she took them off, heard the faint sound of cloth striking the floor.

He knew there was no escape. If nothing else, Marylynn was persistent. He submitted to her, and wound up helping her. Her eagerness became like a contagious fever, and he got caught up in her passion. They made love in silence, except for her moans of pleasure and his own long sigh when he reached the summit. She dug her fingernails into his back and the stars whirled in the sky outside their window until he floated back to earth, sated, his senses drugged to a peacefulness that was almost beyond comprehension. He held her in his arms. Her body quivered as if she was weeping, and he thought perhaps she was, whether out of gratitude, relief, or sorrow that this might be their last time together.

He slept and his dreams were fraught with scenes and images that baffled him. He rode into barren canyons that opened into great gorges that were impassable, and he climbed into complicated terrain where every trail was blocked by more canyons and deep, brush-choked gullies. And when he found a way out, he ran into steep sheer bluffs that rose to the sky and barred him from passage. He awoke in the morning wringing wet from sweat, and for a long time he lay there, wondering where he was.

Then he touched the bare skin of her back and heard her purring breath and knew she was still fast asleep. She reeked of the musk of their lovemaking, and yet her hair was scented like lavender or lilacs, and in the light, her face of repose was beautiful beyond words.

He slid from the bed, tiptoed around the room. He dressed but kept his boots off, carried them from the room along with his rifle and saddlebags. Marylynn did not awaken, and he felt like a thief leaving her like that. But he knew if he didn't leave now, he never would. Before he closed the door, he almost went back, but steeled himself and shook his head.

When he got well away from the room, he stopped and put on his boots, leaning against the wall so that he didn't lose his balance.

He woke up the young Mexican boy who was sleeping in the stables on a pile of straw. The boy, whose name was Eladio, lit a lantern so that Lew could see to saddle Ruben. Lew tipped him a silver dollar and rode out onto the dark street. He rode past the Tecolote, with its wooden owl over its name on the false front, saw that it was quiet, and continued on toward the center of town. A dog barked at him and he saw dark cats slinking across the street and in between the buildings. Somewhere in the distance a cock crowed and a few people showed up on the street, walking to destinations he could not fathom.

He looked at the hotels along the way, then made a circle, riding two blocks off the main road from the east and then circling back until he was in the vicinity of the Tecolote. He looked at the hotels and filed their names away in his mind. He continued his circle to the other side, looking for both hotels and a nondescript livery stable where he could board Ruben and walk to the Tecolote.

He found a hotel a block away from the cantina, on the corner. It was aptly named El Rincon, and it was plain, drab, and cheap. He tied his horse to the hitch rail and walked into an empty lobby. There was a small bell on the counter, and he picked it up and jiggled it. The small tinkle brought a stirring from behind the closed door and a moment later a man emerged, tugging on his suspenders.

His shirt was wrinkled and his thinning hair disheveled. He was in his fifties, a wizened man whose eyes were rheumy and laced with red veins. He reeked of cheap whiskey and stale beans.

"A buck a night, six dollars the week, four bits for a bath, six bits gets you a shave. A dollar six bits gets you a night woman if you don't mind Mexes."

"Just a room," Lew said, plunking three silver dollars down on the counter. "And maybe you have a stable out back, or nearby?"

The man looked up at him, shoved the ledger toward him, and cocked a thumb in the direction of the inkwell and pen.

"You ain't runnin' from the law are you, mister?"

"No. Why?"

"We get owlhoots in here now and again, and the law takes a dim view of us harborin' criminals. They come by ever' once in a while."

"Well, I'm about as unwanted as you can get, if that's any help," Lew said, cracking a smile.

"We got a little ol' barn out back, you're right. But you better tote your tack inside your room. Mexes steal anything what ain't nailed down."

"What about my horse?"

"They hang horse thieves hereabouts. Your horse will be safe, I reckon."

The clerk made change. The coins jingled on the counter.

"The name's Lester," the clerk said. "I'm here sometimes. When I ain't, you got to get by until I get back. They's a privy out back and a pump for your water. You better walk your horse back to the barn. We had a pilgrim ride his back twixt the buildings and the horse spooked, kicked holes in the adobe. I hate to patch adobe. It's like tackin' jelly to a wall."

He handed Lew a key.

"You got room five," he said.

Lew thanked Lester and led Ruben back between the hotel and the pawnshop building next door. The barn was adobe and smelled of dried alfalfa and fermenting corn. He unsaddled and laid his tack out to carry to his room through the back door. He put the horse in an open stall, slipped a halter over his head, and tied the end of the long rope to a post. The horse could move around in the stall and go out, but he wouldn't wander far. And he probably wouldn't get tangled up in the rope. The other stalls were empty, which probably meant the hotel had only him for a guest.

The room was Spartan to an extreme, but it would do, Lew thought. It had a rickety table and a rattan chair to sit in, a cotlike mattress on a bunk frame. Bare walls, a night jar, an empty pitcher and tin cup, and a clay ashtray. The tabletop was marred with cigarette burns, and the flimsy curtains were dusky with smudge and smelled of stale smoke. The window looked out onto the building next door, an adobe with pocked blemishes he assumed were made by a panicky horse's hooves.

He set his saddle, bridle, saddlebags, and rifle on the floor at the foot of the bed and sat on it. The mattress was stuffed with cotton or some other material that was lumpy. The sheets, at least, were clean, and smelled of lye soap.

Lew took off his hat and sailed it onto one of the lumpy pillows. He rubbed his forehead and took in a deep breath.

He looked around the austere room and thought to himself that this was about as far down as a man could get. He had been a fool to leave Marylynn, but he couldn't drag her into his life, a life on the run from the law. He hoped Lester wasn't poring over wanted flyers and putting two and two together. He'd hate to be dragged off to jail or shot for bounty.

This was the kind of place where a man could drop out of sight. He had only one worry at the moment: Charley Grimes. He was likely somewhere in town, and probably keeping an eye out for Lew, to collect the reward. He'd have to deal with Grimes sooner or later.

And somewhere on his backtrail was the U.S. marshal, Blackhawk. If Lew stayed too long in Santa Fe, Blackhawk was bound to catch up with him. But there was Wayne Smith to deal with, too, unless the marshal had captured him in Denver. Smith had a lot to answer for.

He scolded himself for having such thoughts. Why couldn't he just let the world run itself, while he made his way in it? He wasn't the law, and he wasn't a vigilante. Leastways, he didn't think he was.

But there was something in him that drove him to right wrongs. His own experience, perhaps. A sense of justice, honed to a fine edge. Smith was really none of his business. And neither was Grimes, unless he called him out. He should just ride on, disappear, and let whatever law there was take care of those outlaws.

That's what he should do, Lew thought. And knew.

But that's not what he was going to do. He had to know if Smith had gotten away with his robbery in Denver and if he was going to show up in Santa Fe.

He owed Carol that much, he thought.

And maybe he was a vigilante. He was vigilant, that was for sure.

If he wasn't, he knew he would be dead.

14

IT FELT GOOD TO WALK AGAIN, TO USE MUSCLES IN HIS LEGS THAT
had softened some from days on horseback. He walked all
around Santa Fe, looking at the people and the shops, the
busy stores, the vendors and the buyers. By day, the city
pulsed with commerce. Everyone he saw seemed to have a
purpose, all seemed bent on doing business, buying or selling. The carts were laden with everything from firewood to
furniture. He saw silversmiths and whiskey drummers, jewelry makers setting turquoise stones in bracelets and neck-
laces, potters at their wheels with the smell of wet clay
heavy on the air when he poked his head inside their shops,
weavers weaving blankets and serapes and scarves, Indians
selling beads and moccasins on street corners, painters setting out their canvases on homemade wooden easels, scribes
sitting in doorways near the telegraph office, and butchers
batting away flies from the fresh meat on their sturdy
blocks.

He heard half a dozen languages, including Spanish and
German, English, French, and dialects he could not identify.
None paid him any attention, and he thrived on the anonymity,
was able to study faces and watch the pretty Mexican girls
dance, clap his hands with the rest of the throng, and throw

coins on a brightly colored blanket while fiddlers, guitarists, and drummers made music that rang and throbbed with the very heartbeat of the city.

He saw *charros* riding fine-blooded Arabian horses, sitting on silver-studded saddles. He ate spicy adobo and refried beans wrapped in flour tortillas, bought from a boy carrying a cloth-covered basket, and he tasted chocolate that nearly made him giddy with its aroma and flavor. He drank lemonade that cooled him and made his mouth pucker with its sour tang. He tried on turquoise and silver rings and saw handmade boots with their fine tooling that made him regard his own and wonder if he should splurge and buy a pair.

By early afternoon, the pace slowed and many of the shops closed so their owners could take their siestas, and a drowsiness came over him, and a loneliness that was nearly unbearable. He thought of Marylynn and Carol and Seneca, and walked back to his shabby hotel just so people could not see the sadness on his face, nor detect the sorrow inside him for all that might have been, and all that never was.

He slept away the afternoon at his hotel, lulled to sleep by the buzzing of flies, the rumble of carts out on the street, and the mud daubers building a nest outside his window. He slept and dreamed and woke up soaking wet with sweat and felt his beard, which had grown thick and unruly. He wished he could shave it off, but knew he should not. He washed his hair and trimmed it with a straight razor, left his beard to its own shagginess, and bathed in cold water in a tub, scrubbing himself with lye soap and holding up browned hands, looking down at a prison-pale body floating in grimy suds.

He wondered what Marylynn was doing as he dressed and looked out at the puddles of shadow beginning to form on the wall of the pawnshop next door. He tried not to think of her as he cleaned his pistol and oiled the action, slid six cartridges back into the cylinder, practiced his draw for two minutes, and then put polish to his boots and had to wash his hands once again.

He filled an empty flour sack he had in his saddlebags with grain left over from the trip, and he left his room, locking the door.

It was just coming on dusk when Lew walked out the back door of the hotel to check on Ruben in the barn. Crickets sawed their fiddles in the grasses around the barn, and the sky was smeared with smudged clouds banked like the dead hulls of ships against the dark shore of the sky. A faint glow pulsed behind the Sangre de Cristos, salmon and peach coals on a dying fire.

Ruben whickered when Lew entered the barn, and another horse stuck its head out and bleated a long rippling whinny, a small dun that was still wet from being ridden hard. Lew studied it for a moment in the dim light, but did not recognize it as any horse he had seen before. He could not see its brand, but he would remember the horse if he ever saw it again. Its mane was cropped short, and its topknot bobbed. Its ribs were starting to show, and when he lifted its left forefoot, he saw that the shoe was worn down to a thin slice of iron.

The horse had been ridden a long ways, he decided, and was too tired to eat or drink. He patted its withers and saw to Ruben, found that he needed fodder for the night. He emptied the sack into his feed bin and hung it, empty, on a peg outside the stall. Ruben bent his neck and began feeding. Lew filled the water trough from a bucket he found out back next to a rusty pump.

When he returned the empty bucket, his boot struck something that didn't feel right. It wasn't a rock or a stick or a dirt clod, but something yielding like a toadstool or a puffy plant. He looked down and saw a scrap of cloth—canvas, it looked like. He bent down and picked it up. It had writing on it, and as he started to stand up straight, he saw something shiny a foot away. Curious, he stepped over and touched the object. He hefted it and saw that it was a metal bar. It was smooth, but had lettering on its face, lettering that was stamped in. The bar was silver. He stuck it in his pocket and held the scrap of canvas up. He saw the words "Bank," "Denver," and "Leadville." It was, he knew, from a bank bag.

The heavy canvas was grimy, clogged with dirt. The silver bar weighed at least six ounces, he figured.

Someone carrying that bag had snagged it on something and torn a hole in it. The bag had probably been filled with silver bars. Most of those may have fallen to the ground. Whoever had picked them up had missed one, and probably ground the scrap of canvas under his or her boot while picking up the silver bars.

Lew wondered if the dun horse was connected to the bag scrap and the bar of silver.

He walked back to the barn.

He spoke to Ruben and looked at the dun horse again. He figured it hadn't been there ten minutes before he'd come inside. The horse had been unsaddled, but showed no sign of a rubdown, no trace of a brush or curry comb. Someone in a powerful hurry had put the horse up, slipped a halter on it, then left the animal to fend for itself.

None of his business, he thought. But he couldn't walk to the Tecolote carrying a silver bar and that scrap of canvas.

Lew returned to his room, put the bar and piece of bank bag in one of his saddlebags, then walked to the front.

A man stood at the counter, signing the ledger. He looked up as Lew passed by, then turned his attention back to the clerk.

The look had been brief.

The man's face was powdery with dust, his beard at least a week old, and a large sweat circle blackened the left side of his shirt. His boots were dusty, too.

And Lew was sure he had seen the man somewhere before. But where?

Lester looked at Lew in recognition, nodded to him.

"To answer your question, Mr. Baker," Lester said, "Mr. Moon said he'd meet you at the Tecolote Cantina after you got in. Do you need directions to find it?"

"Naw, I know where it is," Baker said, shoving the ledger toward Lester.

"That'll be five bucks," Lester said.

Lew heard the clank of silver dollars on the counter. So Baker was going to stay a few days, Lew thought as he walked out onto the street.

The horse at the hitch rail was lathered. Ropes of foam hung like dirty braids from the horse's neck and chest. It was heaving, its sides expanding and contracting like a black-smith's bellows, wheezing noises issuing from its throat. Across the street, standing in the shadows, was another man, holding his horse. He had a sawed-off shotgun in his hand, his arm dangling by his side. Lew couldn't see his face. The man didn't move. He just stood there, and Lew thought he must be waiting for Baker, had probably ridden in with him. He glanced at Baker's saddlebags, saw that they were bulging, and that from one of them, a scrap of canvas poked out. It looked like the same kind of canvas Lew had stashed away in his room.

He walked to the corner and turned toward the Tecolote, his mind racing. Had he seen Baker someplace before? There was something familiar about the man.

Leadville? Pueblo? Somewhere else?

He didn't recognize the man's face. But there was that feeling of recognition that he couldn't shake.

Maybe, he thought, it would come to him, that night, to-morrow, or sometime.

Baker was going to the Tecolote. Probably the man in the shadows across the street was going there, too. To meet with the man who had ridden the dun horse, a man named Moon. That was all he knew at the moment.

Or was it?

No, he knew a mite more. Charley Grimes might be at the Tecolote, too. That seemed to be a watering hole for criminals. The cantina was where Wayne Smith would be if he escaped from Denver. In fact, Lew thought, maybe Smith was already in Santa Fe. Would he have had time to pull off his robbery in Denver and get to Santa Fe by now? Maybe. It was possible.

Now, as he walked toward the cantina, Lew was glad that he had left Marylynn.

Although he had never been there, Lew knew that the Tecolote was no place for a woman, not the kind of woman Marylynn was.

And maybe, he thought, it was no place for him, either.

If Moon and Baker knew Grimes, along with the man in the shadows, then he was already outnumbered.

Grimes was the only one who knew who Lew was and that he had a price on his head.

Lew's impulse just then was to turn right around and head back to his hotel. That would be the safe thing to do.

But Grimes was connected to Wayne Smith, and Wayne Smith had murdered Carol and her children.

The woman he loved.

There was a price on Smith's head, too. But it wasn't in gold or silver.

It was in blood.

15

U.S. MARSHAL HORATIO BLACKHAWK HATED TO ADMIT DE-
feat. But he had to admit that Wayne Smith had outsmarted
him and the entire posse. It had been with a heavy heart that
he was forced to send a telegram from Denver to the U.S.
marshal in Santa Fe, saying that not only was Wayne Smith
heading there, but he should keep on the lookout for Lew
Wetzel Zane. He knew the marshal assigned to New Mexico, Cordwainer Vogel. Cord was a good man, but he was
probably no match for Wayne Smith. So Blackhawk had
told him to keep his eyes open and wait for his arrival.
He had a hunch that if Vogel found Zane, he'd also find
Smith.

There had been no payroll robbery at the Brown Palace
Hotel. Armed lawmen from both Pueblo and Denver had
been hoaxed by Smith. They had all been at the hotel when
Smith and his men had robbed the Tabor Opera House, steal-
ing an unknown amount of silver that Horace Tabor had hidden in a basement vault. The reason they didn't know how
much silver Smith had taken was because Haw Tabor
wouldn't divulge how much silver he had salted away from
his rich Leadville mines.

Blackhawk had questioned Horace Tabor and his wife, Baby Doe, after the daring robbery.

"Those were the last silver bars from the Matchless," Tabor said. "I was transporting them to my bank here in Denver when the bandits struck."

"You didn't expect this?" Blackhawk asked.

"Horace took precautions," Baby Doe said.

"Yes, I had armed guards, and there was a certain amount of secrecy regarding the transfer."

"Have you ever met Wayne Smith?" Blackhawk asked.

"No, sir," Tabor said. "We never heard of him until you told us. Can you catch him, get my silver back?"

Blackhawk shook his head.

"This was very well planned, sir. Smith had cohorts stationed at various places with fresh horses."

"Like the Pony Express," Tabor said.

"Yes. The posse was hot on his trail south of Denver. But he and his men had fresh horses. The posse did not."

"I'm offering a substantial reward," Tabor said. "I want that silver back."

"Yes, sir. We know where Smith is going. We'll catch him."

"I want to see him hang," Tabor said.

Baby Doe's eyes glittered at her husband's words.

Blackhawk had made no promises regarding punishment. But he knew how powerful Tabor was in Denver. He had come to the plains in '59, bought into some mines, acquired others. People said he had the "Midas touch," except in his case, everything he touched turned to silver. He had built the opera house in Leadville and now had one in Denver. He had bought prime property in downtown Denver, along Sixteenth Street, and was now president of the Denver Chamber of Commerce.

Before he left, Tabor whispered something in Blackhawk's ear.

"That would be quite an honor," Blackhawk said. "I'll do my best."

Blackhawk had no idea how much silver had been stolen, but he gathered that it was a substantial amount. Tabor had

put up a twenty-five-thousand-dollar reward for the return of
the silver bars. That was big money anywhere, but in Denver, it was a small fortune.

Now, Blackhawk was wearing out leather heading for
Santa Fe. In Pueblo, he had met with local law enforcement
officers who had told him a strange tale about bodies found
near Raton Pass.

"We identified a pilgrim, one Rex William Baxter, who
had been traveling with his daughter, Marylynn Baxter,"
Sheriff Alfredo Hernandez had said. "Then we found three
dead men, all shot, who were part of Smith's gang. They had
left fresh horses for Smith and his cronies and were probably
headed for Santa Fe, or another way station to leave more
fresh horses."

"What do you figure?" Blackhawk asked. "Who killed
the outlaws, and do you know who they were?"

"We don't know who killed them. We identified them:
Calvin Weems, Fritz Gunther, and Billy Hatfield. They were
well-known gunnies here in Pueblo. It snowed up there, but
we found plenty of tracks that told us some of the story."

"Let's hear it," Blackhawk said.

"Well, somebody killed Weems where we found Mr. Baxter's body. Whoever killed Weems apparently rescued the
Baxter girl, age about nineteen, near as we can figure. Them
two rode on up the pass, and the other two gunnies jumped
them. Whoever was with Marylynn got off his horse and
went after them. We found their bodies in a place of concealment. Then, whoever shot them rejoined the other person, probably the girl, and they rode on over the pass."

"Anything else?" Blackhawk was in a hurry to get to
Santa Fe, but he wanted as much information as he could get.

"We found a cart that belonged to Baxter. We're still going through it. Mostly household stuff, clothes and such. Pil-
grims ought to know how dangerous that road is sometimes.
Them two shouldn't have been traveling all by their lone-
somes."

"Any idea who the other man was, the one who shot the
Smith men?"

"No, but if you're looking for him, he's riding with that girl. Leading two riderless horses. I figure the outlaws had three mounts. Gal took one to ride, maybe. We figure she got out of that mess alive."

And that was all that Blackhawk knew, but he did pick up the trail south of Raton Pass, learned in Las Vegas that Smith had gotten fresh horses there, and that a man named Jones had registered at a hotel with his wife.

Blackhawk smiled when he looked at the hotel register and saw the name. Ed Jones. He knew that this was the name of Seneca's father. So, he had been right. Lew Zane was still a vigilante. He knew that it was Zane who had rescued Marylynn Baxter and killed those three outlaws. It had to be. And apparently, Zane had taken the girl under his wing.

Benny Rodriguez told Blackhawk about the horses.

"Mister Jones, he sell two horses to Hiram Fogarty."

"Clerk at the hotel said there was another man here. A man named Charley Grimes."

"Oh, yes. Mr. Grimes. He have five horses. He took them somewhere and come back, then ride away."

"What do you mean he took them somewhere?" Blackhawk asked.

"He buy a lot of food and some grain. He take the horses away. I don't see them no more."

"Where do you think he took them?"

"Maybe he sell them someplace."

"What did Grimes want with Mr. Jones?"

"He say those horses Jones have belong to friends. He look at the brands."

"And this Grimes let Jones sell two horses to Fogarty?"

"Yes. Jones tell Grimes he knows his friends and they have new horses."

So, Blackhawk thought, Zane talked himself out of that one. Grimes must be one of Smith's men who furnished fresh horses. Five horses. So Wayne expected to have four men with him. What about those Zane killed? Were they supposed to be riding with Smith?

The puzzle was getting more complicated. But at least he had a line on Zane and the Baxter girl, and they, too, seemed to be headed for Santa Fe.

When he rode into Glorieta, Blackhawk knew, somehow, that the Baxter girl and Zane would stop there, even if it was only to buy more food. The town was small enough for him to cover it and not lose much time. He was elated to find that a pair matching their description had passed through, and, at the café, he got more than he bargained for when he questioned the waitress and cook.

"So, Lupita," Blackhawk said, over a cup of coffee at the counter, "you recognized Lew Wetzel Zane when he was in here?"

"He had the beard, but he looked like the drawing on the paper, yes."

"And there was a fight?"

"Yes. The cook, Pedro, he try to capture this outlaw."

"And what happened?"

"The girl who was with this Zane, she took his gun and said she would shoot me. I had the shotgun, but I put it down."

"And then what?"

"Pedro, he stop fighting. Zane and the girl, they rode away. This Zane, he take a flyer with him when he go."

So Zane knew about the reward.

No trace of Smith and his men. Blackhawk figured he must be avoiding the main road, traveling cross country with his henchmen and the silver.

He rolled a smoke after leaving the café and rode out of Glorieta toward Santa Fe.

Zane could not know how much danger he was in. If he was planning to avenge Carol Smith's death, he'd be out-gunned and outnumbered.

Yes, Zane was a wanted man. And Blackhawk was bound to take him back to Arkansas to stand trial.

But he was rooting for Lew Zane.

He had always had a soft spot for the underdog.

And, right now, Lew Wetzel Zane was in more trouble than the law could throw on top of him.

Somehow, he had to find Zane before Zane found Wayne Smith.

What happened to Lew Zane shouldn't be any of his business, Blackhawk thought. Smith was a much more dangerous man and should be his highest priority. But he was damned if he'd let Zane get eaten alive by a pack of wild dogs.

16

MARYLYNN SOAKED IN THE OAK TUB A LONG TIME AFTER SHE had scrubbed herself and washed her hair. She had awakened early, before dawn, her hands splayed and reaching out, touching the bed sheets, the pillows, searching for Lew in the dark. But she knew he was gone before she ever summoned the courage to arise and face the empty room.

She almost couldn't believe that he would leave her. Were all men that way? Cold, unfeeling? Did not they have the same fires burning in them that she had? Her whole body sizzled with an electric burning at the sound of his voice. And when he touched her, no matter how slight the touch, or where on her body, she melted inside as if he had turned her molten. His kisses still burned on her lips, on her breasts, her tummy, and down between her thighs. When she closed her eyes, she could smell his manly scent, and when she opened them, she half expected him to be there, come back because of a longing inside him that was as unbearable as her own.

She emerged from the tub like some golden nymph as the morning sun shot shafts of light through the slatted windows. The water on her body glistened like crushed diamonds and silvery motes danced in the air as she wrapped herself in a towel and rubbed it over her sleek skin. Her hair hung in wet ringlets, like small ropes, and she rubbed hard to remove all the moisture. In her room, she dressed, despite her annoyance at putting on dirty clothes, clothes she had pounded and flapped to get the dust out of, but that still reeked of the desert and were heavy with its grit.

She knew what she was going to do that day, had planned it all out while she was soaking in the tub. She gathered up the Colt .45, holster, and gunbelt and wrapped it into a bundle and slipped it into one of the pillowcases. She went to the desk and told the clerk, a man she had never seen before, that she wished to pay for a week's stay.

"You done paid for a week, missus. Did you want another week?"

"No. I—I'll decide later," she said.

She hadn't known that Lew had paid her bill in advance. He must have done it when he left that morning. She struggled with the thought that there might be a hidden message in that act, but everything she came up with sounded ridiculous to her. Did that mean he was coming back, or that he wanted a week's head start to put distance between them?

She ate breakfast in a little café on Ruiz Street, chorizo and huevos rancheros with a green chili sauce and a glass of goat's milk. By that time, Santa Fe was all abustle, and she was fascinated as she walked along, looking at the faces of the Indians and Mexicans, the few white people who were out and about. She stopped in stores that sold dresses and looked at the clothing the other women wore. She went to a hardware store, Finch's, on Calle Segundo, barely glancing at the merchandise. A woman stood behind the counter, her sturdy full body encased in a flowery dress, her hair streaked with gray and tied back in a bun. She looked Germanic, Marylynn thought, with her heavy features and thick neck.

Marylynn plopped the heavy pillowcase down on the counter.

"Do you sell guns here?" she asked.

"Guns?"

"I want to buy a pistol. A pistol a lady might carry."

"Ah, no. We have some old rifles. No pistols."

"Can you tell me where I might buy a pistol?"

"Do you want a new pistol, or one that has been used?"

"Well, I don't want to pay a lot of money for one, and I have one to trade."

"Ah, then you must go to a pawnshop, maybe. I will tell you where there is one that sells pistols. It is not far. It's called Tesoro Pawnbrokers, It's right next to the El Rincon Hotel."

"If you would be kind enough to give me directions . . ."

"Most certainly. I must say, a young thing like yourself shouldn't be fooling with guns."

"Ah, it's for my brother."

"Oh, I see."

The lady gave Marylynn directions to the pawnshop.

She meant to go right there, but there were so many shops, she began stopping in each one. She tried on dresses and pants, boots and handwoven shawls. She bought a pair of riding pants that fit snugly on her hips. Then she selected stout boots and a wide-brimmed hat. In another shop, she bought a plain dress that was form-fitting. She remembered Lew's words about wearing clothing that would not interfere with her ability to draw and shoot a pistol.

It was late in the day, almost dark, when she began looking for Tesoro Pawnbrokers.

She found it easily enough as the sun's rays were waning, and stood there for a moment in shadow, looking in the window at all the watches, field glasses, pistols, rifles, pots and pans, knives and jewelry, rings and bracelets, concho belts, and trade blankets.

Out of the corner of her eye, she saw a man emerge from the hotel. Startled, she stepped into the recessed doorway and stared at Lew Zane emerging from the hotel. To conceal her face, she hefted the bundles in her arms, the goods she had bought wrapped in paper and tied tight with twine, the pillowcase resting heavy against her stomach. She stifled a gasp and her heart began beating with a faster pace. She felt her blood pound in her ears.

She saw him cross the street, glancing at a man standing by a horse. The man held a sawed-off shotgun at his side. Lew appeared not to have noticed the armed man, but she knew he had. She knew him well enough by now to know that he would notice such a man.

Someone came to the door while she was standing there.

"We're closing in five minutes," a man said.

Marylynn gasped and turned around at the unexpected sound of his voice.

"No, wait," she said. "I'm coming in."

"Hurry it up," the man said. "You hiding from somebody, young lady?"

She slipped into the store and let the bundles fall away from her face.

"No . . . I—I just . . ."

"Never mind. You see something in the winder you wanted?"

He was a florid-faced man with a large bulbous nose, a pinched mouth, a razor-thin moustache that looked as if it had been drawn with a charcoal pencil, and sideburns that fanned out at the bottoms like chisels. He wore a blue chambray shirt and striped trousers, and suspenders that cut into his shoulders like freight straps. His shoes were scuffed and unshined, a pale shade of brown.

"No. I mean, I don't know. I want to purchase a pistol and I have a six-gun to trade, a Colt."

"Let's see what you have, then we can look at what you want. Follow me back to the counter, young lady."

Marylynn bristled. The man couldn't have been much over thirty himself. She knew condescension when she saw it.

She laid the pillowcase on the glass-topped counter and slid from it the pistol with its gunbelt coiled around it.

"Yep, that's a Colt, all right," the man said. "In .45 caliber?"

"Yes."

"Loaded?"

"I, uh, yes."

"Dangerous to bring a loaded pistol into a commercial establishment such as this," he said. "Step back and I'll take a look."

Marylynn took a half step backward, away from the counter, and the man unwound the gunbelt and slid the Colt from its holster. He opened the gate and put the hammer on half cock. He ejected all six cartridges, which fell on a felt pad he slipped under them so they didn't rattle when they struck.

He took a small cotton wad from a box on the counter and tucked it into one of the cylinders. Then he held the pistol up to the strongest light available and peered down the barrel. He sniffed and made sucking sounds with his mouth that made him seem like an asthmatic.

"All right. It's clean, anyways, and the barrel seems to be okay. Action works. Trigger pull not too strong. Double action, which is good. How much do you want for it?"

"I—I'm not sure. I want to buy, trade that is, for a small-caliber pistol. Something a young boy might use."

"Well, let me show you what I have," the man said, and started pulling out drawers. He laid four pistols out in front of her on the felt cloth. Two of them were single shot, a third was a double-barreled derringer, and the fourth was a Smith & Wesson in .32 caliber.

"Them are what I got," he said.

She picked up the Smith & Wesson. It felt good in her hand. She pulled the trigger several times. Cocked the hammer back by hand. She held the empty pistol up and stuck out her arm, sighting down the barrel. She pulled the trigger again. The hammer struck with a loud click that made the man wince every time she did it.

"Barrel cracks open to load in cartridges," he said.

"Do you have a box of ammunition to go with it? A holster?"

"I think we can find a holster for it. Might not have a cartridge belt for bullets that small. And I got a couple of boxes of .32 ammunition."

The pistol fit the holster. The man set two boxes of cartridges on the counter.

"I'll take both boxes," she said. "And the pistol and holster."

The man smacked his lips, made sucking sounds with them. He tapped his temple with a bony finger. He picked up the Colt again, then slid it back in its holster.

"I'll take the trade and give you two dollars," he said.

"I should get more. The Colt is a better gun," she said.

"Two dollars and four bits, then," the man said, a curt whip to his voice.

"Three dollars," she said.

"Umm, I don't know."

"Look, how many of these small pistols do you sell? This one looks dusty to me."

"All right. I'm closing up. Three dollars and not a penny more, miss."

She cracked the pistol and opened one of the boxes of cartridges.

"I prefer you not load that pistol in here," he said, opening a drawer and fishing out three one-dollar bills. He set them on the counter.

"Don't worry," she said. "I'm not going to shoot you."

She filled all six cylinders, closed the barrel.

"That's a double action," he said. "Be careful."

"I know it's double action, sir," she said, and snatched up the three bills and stuck them all wadded up in her bodice. She put the new pistol in the pillowcase and folded the cloth tightly, wrapping it around the gun. "Thank you, sir."

"You be careful with that pistol, young lady," the man called out as she strode to the door. "Say, you're not going to shoot anybody, are you?"

She didn't turn around, nor did she answer.

She could hear the man's mouth make suckling noises as she opened the door and stepped back out on the street.

The man with the shotgun was gone, and so was his horse. The street was empty, darkening with shadows. She held her bundles tightly under her arms and walked rapidly away, heading back to her hotel.

So now she knew where Lew was probably staying. At El Rincon Hotel. Unless he had been there to see a woman, or someone else. She wondered where he was going at that time of day. Her heart pounded fast in her chest when she thought of him, so close and yet so far.

She stopped suddenly and turned around. She walked briskly toward El Rincon. Perhaps Lew was staying there, and perhaps the clerk might know where he was going. She had to know. Even though she felt like a thief, or worse, she had to know.

What was it her father had said to her once? "Don't never give up if there's something you really want." That was it. And something else, too. "Nothing sadder than what might have been. You see opportunity, you go after it."

Well, she had seen Lew Zane, and they had been intimate. She wanted him.

She was going after him, come hell or high water.

She tightened her lips together, a look of determination on her face.

"Persistence," she told herself, "is my middle name."

The night came on, plunging the street into darkness. She saw the pawnbroker hurrying away up the street. Lamplight shone through the hotel window, and she shivered from the sudden chill.

But deep inside her, there was warmth.

The warmth of hope.

17

ZANE WAITED OUTSIDE THE TECOLOTE, STANDING IN THE SHAD-
ows, listening to the ebb and flow of conversation inside.
The talk was subdued, friendly, and in both Spanish and English. From what he heard, those inside seemed to be mostly
ranchers or ranch hands, drovers, laborers, and workers in
various professions speaking quietly of their trades or the
weather, their wives and gal friends. Such talk, he thought,
might have sounded the same in the Osage general store or
around any cracker barrel in any number of small towns he'd
passed through.

Horses were tied up on both sides of the street, their reins
wrapped around hitch rails or through hitch rings. A wagon
stood farther up the street, with two Missouri mules in harness. There was the sound of switching tails and low whick-
ers. Laughter bubbled up inside the cantina, and glasses
clinked like far-off bells oddly out of tune. The dark sky glittered with stars flung like crushed diamonds across black
felt, and off in the distance a dog barked, then went silent.

Three men rode toward him from the far end of the street.
They turned their horses in at an empty spot with a hitching
post and a rail outside a dry goods store and next to a store
with a sign on it that announced *ABARROTES*, which appeared

to be part of the same deserted building. Their low voices drifted his way, and presently, after securing their mounts, they walked toward the cantina.

Lew held himself motionless in a well of shadow until they passed, then fell in behind them. He knew that he was less likely to be noticed if he entered with other men. He hadn't been able to see any of their faces, but from the way they walked, he was sure that he did not know them.

None greeted the men who walked in, but they were accepted, and so was Lew, who made his way to the nearest opening at the bar. A few men glanced at him, but none showed surprise. He sat on a bar stool and did not draw attention to himself.

Lew glanced around to see what the others at the bar were drinking. The air was tainted with the odor of tequila and mescal, but he sniffed the tang of whiskey, too, and some of the men were drinking sudsy beers. Blue and gray smoke hung in a lazy pall over the main room and its tables. Far in the back, where brighter lanterns shone, men sat playing poker on tables covered with green felt, and the clatter of chips sounded like false teeth clacking together.

One of the barkeeps sauntered over to him after pouring drinks for the three men who had come in ahead of him.

"Whiskey," Lew ordered, looking the man straight in the eye.

"Con agua o derecho?" the man said.

"Derecho. No agua."

The barkeep smiled. He brought a shot glass and a bottle, poured the glass to the brim. Lew laid a silver dollar next to the bottle, and the man slid it away into his palm as if he were a magician used to sleight of hand. He returned and laid four bits in change next to the glass of whiskey. *"Gracias, amigo,"* the man said and smiled again.

Lew nodded, but did not smile. He touched the shot glass to his lips, but only let a small amount seep onto them. He glanced up at the large mural on the wall behind the bar. The painting depicted a small mariachi band in the background and a man and woman dancing in the foreground, with spectators looking on, smiling. The woman's breasts were pronounced and protruding from her red and yellow blouse. The man wore tight black trousers, an open gaucho shirt, and a flat-crowned black hat. The woman had long black hair with a blue flower attached to one side. Everyone in the portrait was smiling, and some of the men were pouring beer from a keg into cups. One or two held bottles in their hands or tipped up, their lips touching the necks. Lew supposed the mural made a man want to drink, get married, or dance, only one of which was probably allowed in the Tecolote.

The murals on the other walls depicted alluring women in various stages of nudity and seminudity, sprawled on couches or beds, holding up Spanish fans or caressing some handsome bare-chested Don Juan. These were less garishly lit by lamplight, but were visible nonetheless.

He turned slightly and surveyed the dimly lit room, spacious enough, he figured, to hold nearly a hundred people. He reckoned there were thirty or forty at tables, with several empty ones among them, another dozen or so at the long oak bar, which had been polished to a high sheen. He did not recognize anyone in the room. Certainly Grimes was not there, which helped him relax enough to actually sip some of the whiskey. It tasted of charred oak and brine and had a bite to it that warmed his throat and made his stomach double up into a fist when the liquid reached that level.

The two men nearest him were talking about hauling freight to Taos that week and how much they hated that "dirty little Injun town." Next to them, two Mexicans were talking about their wives and recounting how many children they had.

Lew noticed a newspaper being pushed along the top of the bar from the far end to where he sat, and each man dipped into it, ate something, then shoved it down to the next man. When it got to him, he saw that, atop the crumpled and greasy newspaper were several smoked fish, each one cut in half lengthwise. He picked up a chunk with two fingers and chewed it.

The bartender walked up to him.

"*Troucha*," he said.

"Muy sabroso," Lew said, and took another bite, slipping the smoked meat from the delicate bones of the trout.

A man came up and took the trout from the bar and offered it to the nearest table. The men seated there all dipped their fingers into the meat and pulled up chunks.

Lew decided that the Tecolote was a friendly place. The three bartenders were alert and efficient, and two waiters kept up with their tables. There were no women to be seen.

He took another drink and, out of the corner of his eye, saw two men enter the cantina. The first one he did not recognize, but the second was the man he knew as Baker. They seemed oddly out of place, at first, with their hard faces and shifty dark eyes. A lone man at a table stood up and beckoned to them. The two walked toward him. The three shook hands, and Baker slapped the man on the back. The three sat down. Lew figured this was the man, Moon, they had come to meet. Moon, if that was his name, seemed genuinely glad to see Baker and the other man. They all seemed like old friends. Baker and his companion sat facing the door, and blended in almost immediately.

A waiter stopped at their table and took their order. Lew watched as the waiter returned with two glasses of beer and a bottle of whiskey, along with two shot glasses. Baker paid the waiter, while the other man drank half the beer in his glass, then started looking around the room. Moon and the nameless man conversed in private, their heads bowed, almost touching. Lew could not hear a word under the hum of the other conversations. Baker continued to glance up at the door every now and then, as if he was expecting someone. Probably Grimes, Lew thought.

One of the men sitting nearest him spoke of his wife, who had died of consumption, and of the daughter he was raising with the help of a single neighbor lady. The other man said he ought to marry the neighbor, and the widower shook his head and said that she was fat and could never replace his Clara, and the talk drifted to hauling sacks of corn and lumber to Taos, while Lew finished his drink and ordered another, wondering why he sat there in such an alien place, listening to other people recounting their ordinary lives, while he was an outcast, a hunted man, with no home and no job.

He thought of Seneca and was homesick, a little giddy from the whiskey, even with the trout in his stomach and another newspaper floating down the bar to him. And then he thought of Marylynn and became as lonely as the other men in the cantina, and wondered why so many men said they drank to forget a woman, when the whiskey dredged up thoughts of every woman who walked the earth, the known and the unknown.

He watched Baker and the other man drink their whiskey and down two more beers, and by then he knew he could not down another whiskey or he'd look onto a spinning room and throw up the smoked trout he had eaten.

He shoved his empty glass out of the way, took a deep gulp of air, and started to rise from the bar stool.

That's when Charley Grimes pushed open the batwing doors and entered the cantina.

Lew froze as Grimes looked straight at him.

Then, to his surprise, Grimes looked away and scanned the room as he took another step inside. Baker raised his arm and Grimes spotted him, then strode to the table.

While Grimes was walking across the room, Lew changed his mind and sat back down. When the bartender came over and pointed to his empty glass, Lew shook his head.

"*No mas,*" he said. "*Cerveza, por favor.*"

The bartender removed the shot glass, drew a beer from a keg, and set the foaming glass in front of Lew. Lew paid him, and left the change on the bartop.

He watched the four men who were huddled together over the table. A waiter brought Grimes a beer and an empty shot glass. Grimes poured whiskey into the shot glass, drank it down, and then drank from the glass of beer.

A voice broke Lew's concentration.

"You a stranger here?"

Lew looked at the man nearest him, the one whose wife had died of consumption.

"Just passing through," Lew said.

"What's your trade? Or are you lookin' for work?"

"I mostly do odd jobs," Lew said, trying to think of some trade he might mention.

"Freight office is lookin' for a loader. Hard work, but pays pretty well."

"I might look into it," Lew said, distracted from his observation of the table where the four hard cases sat.

"You come on by Harmon's Freight over on Mercado Street tomorrow morning, about six," the man said.

Lew lifted his glass and drank with a gesture that said thank you.

The man turned back to his companion.

While Lew was talking to the freighter, Grimes kept looking over at Lew.

Lew finished some of the beer and then got up. He left his change for the barkeep and was halfway out the batwing doors when he felt a hand on his shoulder.

"Hey you, mister, hold up a minute," a voice boomed in his ear.

Lew turned and stared into the face of Charley Grimes.

"Yeah?"

"Don't I know you from someplace?" Grimes said.

"Naw, I don't think so."

"You look mighty familiar."

"Not me," Lew said.

"Well, I'm pretty good at faces."

"I never been here before," Lew drawled, changing not only his accent, but the pitch of his voice.

"I'll sure as hell remember directly," Grimes said. "Maybe later, eh?"

"Yeah," Lew said, and stepped outside. Grimes looked at him for a long moment, then went back inside the cantina, furrows appearing on his brow like the tracks of snakes in a layer of putty.

Lew strode away from the saloon and into the smokeless air. He breathed deep and leaned against the wall of the Tecolote for a long moment, as if to let the cobwebs in his brain drift away in the fresh air.

Close call, he thought. Then he wondered why he had come to the Tecolote in the first place. He knew before he went that he would probably run into Grimes, and he knew Baker would probably be there. These men didn't matter to him except that they were a connection to Wayne Smith. Smith was the man he wanted to see—face to face. He wanted to look into the heart of a man who could coldly murder his wife and children for thirty pieces of silver, or many thousand pieces of silver.

He wanted to see what a bastard like that looked like up close with the snout of a six-shooter shoved in his face.

But he already knew. He had seen that same look in the faces of Wiley Pope and Fritz Canby, the boys who had slaughtered his mother and father. He had seen into their hearts and seen greed and lust and something nobody could describe—a coldness, a lack of feeling for mankind.

And in their faces and in their hearts he had seen something else, too. Or rather, he had not seen something else.

A soul.

Lew launched himself away from the wall and headed back toward El Rincon.

That's when he heard something that froze him in his tracks before he even knew for sure what it was.

Boots pounded on the hardwood floor of the cantina. Louder and louder, closer and closer to those batwing doors.

But he knew what it was.

Grimes had remembered who he was.

And now he was coming for him, to collect that thousand-dollar reward.

For a long second, an eternal moment, Lew didn't know whether to run or to turn and face what might be one man or four.

Then, the batwing doors swung wide, outward toward the street.

And there was no more time to think.

18

CHARLEY GRIMES BURST THROUGH THE BATWING DOORS. THE doors screamed on their hinges, like a dozen tortured bats taking wing. In his wake, the cantina fell into a hush that seemed as if all the air had been sucked out of the room.

Lew knew he would stand no chance if he stayed in that spot to fight it out with Grimes. In seconds, other men, smelling blood, would come pouring out of the cantina, and among them, the three who were cronies of Grimes.

Lew ran straight down the dark street, then cut between two buildings and raced to the back alley. Behind him, he could hear pounding boot heels coming after him, faster and faster.

He ran down the alley without looking back over his shoulder, into the stygian darkness, pumping his legs like oiled pistons, stretching his leaps like a bounding gazelle. He breathed through his nose, filling his lungs, drawing energy from oxygen, strength from the fear balling up in his stomach like a fist of molten iron.

"You hold up there, feller, or I'll shoot," Grimes called out behind Lew.

Lew kept running to the end of that alley, then rounded the corner onto another street. He dashed across it, ducking his head to lessen his silhouette. He expected to hear a pistol shot at any moment. When he reached the shadows of a building, he glanced over his shoulder to see Grimes barreling around the corner. He thought he saw a pistol in his hand.

Lew froze against the building, blending into the dark shadow. He stayed motionless until he saw Grimes stop and look up the street. Lew's breath was a whistle through his nostrils. His chest rose and fell like a balloon with a pinhole in it, up and down, as if his lungs would not fill. He hoped Grimes could not hear his breathing from that distance.

"I know who you are, Zane. Might as well give up."

Lew hugged the building, unmoving.

Grimes started walking his way, looking on both sides of the street. He took his time, as if he knew Lew hadn't had time to go very far. Lew could feel his muscles tighten, his nerves begin to clang warning signals in his brain.

One step, pause. Another step, wait. Look. Another step, and Grimes was getting closer.

How good were his eyes in the dark?

Lew did not know.

He edged toward the end of the building. A pair of mannequins inside the glass display window stood in eerie shadow gazing outward. They looked almost like real people in the dim light. Lew took another cautious step.

Grimes stopped and whirled, his gun hand swinging toward Lew.

Lew ducked as Grimes squeezed the trigger. Orange flame belched from the barrel of the pistol. The glass behind Lew shattered, and he heard the bullet thunk into one of the mannequins. The mannequin teetered on its moorings, but did not fall.

Lew ran into the passageway between that building and the next. Another shot rang out, and he heard the splatter of adobe as the bullet nicked the edge of the building.

He did not stop, but ran to the end of the passageway, hit the alley, and veered to his left. He heard running footsteps on the street. He kept running, to the next block, then dashed in between two buildings, puffing hard.

He strained to hear the running footsteps. They stopped when Grimes reached the street. Lew could picture Grimes looking both ways, searching for any sign of him, any movement.

"Zane, you son of a bitch," Grimes yelled, and his voice carried down the street like the last of an echo.

Lew regained his breath and his pulse stopped racing. His heart was pounding, still, but he was not going to move. He drew his pistol and eased back the hammer. If Grimes showed himself in that corridor, he was a dead man.

"I'll get you yet, you bastard," Grimes yelled, and Lew knew he had not moved from his last position.

"Come on," Lew whispered to himself, knowing Grimes could not hear him.

He heard footsteps moving away from him. Angry stomps from Grimes's boots as he left the street.

Another close call, Lew thought. He eased the hammer back down and slid the Colt into its holster. But still, he waited, just in case Grimes snuck back.

He waited five minutes. Ten.

He had no idea where he was, but he started edging along the wall to the next street, opposite the direction from which he had come. Once he got his bearings, he would go back to the hotel and get some sleep. He didn't know if Baker could identify him to Grimes, but he thought not. Still, he knew he would have to be careful. And he might have to move to another hotel in the morning, just to be sure Baker had not made the connection.

He didn't give a damn about Grimes, but he was a thorn in Lew's side. Grimes wanted that bounty money. But Lew wanted Wayne Smith, and those four men in the Tecolote were the bait. If he could keep an eye on them, sooner or later they would meet up with Smith, if Smith was still alive and showed up in Santa Fe.

Lew emerged onto the other street, an unfamiliar street, unlit. The dust was painted with a silver sheen of moonlight, glinted with tiny stars of mica. He angled left to try and get his bearings, thinking he would eventually circle around and come back to El Rincon.

As he moved toward the cross street, he heard a voice call out that sent a shiver up his spine, made his blood leap to his temples as his heart jumped.

"Charley, you get him?"

"Naw, Kip. But I know where he went."

"We'll help you find the bastard."

"Moon and Riley with you?"

"Yeah, they're back there," the other man said, and now Lew knew who it was. Kip Baker. A first name to go with the last. And Riley must have been the man standing guard with the shotgun when Baker was checking into the hotel. Moon stayed there, too, and was the man waiting at the table in the Tecolote when Lew first entered.

"Hey Freddie, over here," Baker yelled. "Bring Jethro with you."

So, now, Lew knew the names of all the men waiting for Smith. Kip Baker, Freddie Moon and Jethro Riley.

"He went up twixt them two buildings yonder," Grimes said, his voice carrying on the night air. "I might have winged him."

"We can get him," Baker said. "Freddie and Jethro can flank him on the cross streets. We'll flush him out."

Lew heard their voices drop as they outlined their strategy, he supposed. He was already moving closer to the cross street, but he knew he couldn't double back there toward the street where the Tecolote stood. He'd have to move in the opposite direction, and fast.

There was a chance that Baker knew he was staying at the hotel. If so, that made his return dangerous.

Lew's thoughts raced as he angled down the next street. A sign identified it as Mariposa, but that didn't help him.

The buildings there were dark, and it was hard to read the signs that identified them. One of them seemed to be a warehouse of some sort, and next to it was what looked like a land office. All adobes, and all dark. He ran across the street to the far side, trying to muffle the sound of his boots.

Off to his left, he heard a man running. That would be either Moon or Riley, hoping to cut him off. Behind him, far down the street he had just vacated, he knew the other man would be running down it to block his escape from that part of town.

Baker and Grimes were running between the two buildings where he had just passed. He heard their footfalls grow louder, and then he knew they were on the street. Well, he thought, unless they were very good trackers, they wouldn't know where he had gone. But they were too close for comfort.

Lew slid between two buildings and headed for the back alley off of Mariposa Street.

The footsteps grew louder and he knew that Grimes and Baker were coming up Mariposa. On the run.

"Which way?" Baker said, his voice loud enough for Lew to hear him.

"This way," Grimes said, and Lew had no idea what he meant.

But as he crept between the two buildings, he knew. Baker and Grimes were right behind him, out on Mariposa Street. He trotted back to the alley, trying not to make much noise, but as soon as he got there, he heard more footsteps, someone running toward him from another direction. The other flanker, he reasoned. He could not go left, he could only go right. He began to run, and the air was heavy in his chest. His lungs were so sore he felt as if he were breathing lead, not air.

Lew reached the other street and turned left. The blur of buildings as he ran were shops, he figured from just what he could see of them out of the corners of his eyes. The darkness helped him, and he stayed close to the buildings on his left. Anyone coming around the corner from the alley would have less of a chance of seeing him right away. But now he knew he had three men coming after him who were not very far away. Where the fourth man was, he had no idea, but he would probably be closing in at some point.

There were no streetlamps, no gaslights nor oil burners. Just the moon above him, big and bright, like a searchlight beaming down on him. The street was wide and long. When he reached the next street, he paused for just an instant.

"There he is," Grimes yelled, and someone fired a shot.

The bullet whizzed by, a split second before Lew heard the report, and he heard it thud into a corner building across the street.

Which way to run?

If he turned left, he might run into the third man. If he turned right, he'd be a target for a long time until he reached the other side of the street. Which way? But he had to run, and fast now. He heard them coming, Baker and Grimes, their boots sounding like a herd of cattle on the run.

Lew ran straight ahead, crossed the street, and started looking for a place to hide. The buildings were packed close together and he could see no opening.

More shops, small ones, were packed together so tightly it seemed like he was facing one long adobe wall.

He turned left, glancing on both sides of the street to see if there was any space between buildings. Ahead of him, he thought he saw a shadow moving across the street. He wondered if that was the other flanker, or just an illusion.

A cat raced out of a doorway and crossed his path. Lew thought his heart had failed for a moment. His lungs were starting to burn, and he drew breath in through both his mouth and nostrils.

"There he goes," Baker yelled.

Then, Grimes called out, "Moon, he's comin' straight at you."

"I see him," Moon yelled back, and Lew knew that the shadow that had crossed the street was the flanker on that side.

But he couldn't see the man anymore. Where in hell was Moon?

Two men behind him, one in front of him. And another somewhere beyond, probably closing in from that direction.

Lew saw a flash of orange flame up the street, and heard the bullet like the whispering cough of a huge bull. The bullet struck the ground a few feet in front of him and spat dirt and grit into his face.

Then more shots came from behind him. One, two, three, as Baker and Grimes pulled the triggers on their double actions.

Bullets fried the air, sizzling past his ears like angry hornets. He drew his pistol, cocked it, and ran to his left, looking for any building that was recessed from the street, any niche he could get into so that he could fire back and defend himself.

Bullets kicked up dirt all around him. Orange flames sprouted hideous flowers from the snouts of pistol barrels. Time seemed to slow to a crawl, like some crippled animal on its last legs.

Lew reached the other side. He smelled fruit, all kinds of fruit, and the musty smell was coming from one of the store fronts. He stumbled onto a door and pushed against it. He could feel the wooden bar give on the other side. One bar, maybe two. He couldn't break in and escape through that door.

He saw Moon, then, or the man he figured to be Moon. He was at the corner, on the opposite side of the street.

He turned and saw two shadows slinking up the street, Baker and Grimes.

Lew hunched down and slid along the storefronts toward Moon. There were no openings between the different *tiendas*.

He was trapped, unless he could find an open door, or a window he could break through.

"We got him," Grimes yelled.

"Moon?" Baker called.

"I see the son of a bitch," Moon yelled, and Lew saw Moon separate from the shadows and angle across the intersection, sure of himself, coming on like a deadly wraith, the pistol in his hand gleaming with moonlight, shooting off sparks like some shooting star gliding through space.

Lew knew he could probably shoot Moon. But then Grimes and Baker would be right on top of him, guns blazing like rockets at a Fourth of July picnic.

Time struggled in its harness like a flapping bird caught in a net.

And, for Lew, there wasn't much of it left.

19

OUT OF THE CORNER OF HIS EYE, LEW SAW SOMETHING FLASH. IT was just a brief flicker, almost unnoticeable. But he was desperate and noticed everything. He turned and saw a pane of glass a foot or two away from him. Bright colors, dulled by the darkness, leaked through the glass and were visible. He slid along the adobe, scraping his shoulder blade against the brick, feeling the granules against the back of his shirt.

He saw framed paintings, blown glass objects, small statues, a velvet throw, and a sign on the window that read ART GALLERY. Without thinking, Lew took three steps away from the window, bent down, and rushed the pane, his shoulder lowered like that of a charging bull. As shots rang out all around him, he smashed through the glass and smacked into an overstuffed chair. The tinkle of glass resounded in his ears, and he felt a sharp, searing pain in his shoulder. He touched his neck and felt hot, wet blood.

But he was in one piece. Glass continued to fall from the cracked window as he dashed through the gallery, past paintings on the wall, statues he dodged on the hardwood floor, and glass cases filled with handmade jewelry, ceramic pottery, and colorful throws made of fine cloth. He heard shouted voices outside on the street, but continued his headlong flight through the store until he came to a back room where there were high shelves with more paintings stacked against them, as well as statues and trinkets. He stirred up choking dust and struggled to breathe. Blood trickled down his face, and his sleeve was wet and dripping. He groped for the back door in the darkness, felt the latch. He rattled and shook the latch until it released and he stumbled onto a small loading dock and a welcome rush of fresh air.

He leaped down the dock and into the alley. He heard, faintly, the clump of boots on the hardwood floors, bewildered shouts and muffled curses as men made their way through the art gallery. He could hear them smashing wood and stone and ceramics as he raced down the alley, his lungs on fire, burning on fresh oxygen.

He crossed a street and kept on running as though his life depended on it. And he knew his life did depend on it. He eased the hammer down on his pistol and slid it back in its holster, jammed it down tight. On and on he raced, back in the direction of both the cantina and the hotel. He didn't veer or swerve, but held to a straight path while a phrase he had learned in school kept repeating itself over and over in his mind. "A straight line is the shortest distance between two points."

Distance was what he needed, and he ran as he had never run before, with his lungs burning like parchment over an open flame. He felt his legs go numb and forced himself to think of fresh blood pumping into them, shooting energy and strength into every fiber, every muscle, every tendon. He ran without seeing, blindly, down one dark alley then another. Dogs and cats yelped and yowled, scattered before him like leaves blown by a passing wind.

Finally, exhausted, he ran between two buildings, into a narrow passageway. He stopped, panting for breath, and leaned against a cool adobe wall. He bent over and put his hands on his knees to hold himself up while he pulled air into his tortured lungs. From far off, he heard faint music and ribbons of voices floating on the night air, unintelligible streamers of disembodied conversation that could have been in a foreign tongue or any number of languages.

He heard air whistling through his nose, felt it wheeze into his lungs and back out again. It was hard work staying alive, he thought. Damned hard work, the hardest he had ever done.

He stood up straight and felt his side. His shirt was torn and there was blood on his skin. He felt along a furrow and knew the wound was not deep. He touched his forehead and winced at the slight pain. His fingers came away sticky with blood. A scratch there, too. But he was no longer bleeding much and he felt no pain. His lungs began to heal, the flames subsiding, the fire banking with each new slow breath. His heart, too, was no longer racing like a scared deer in his chest. His temples no longer pounded or throbbed.

And it was quiet. Blessedly quiet. The laughter and the talk died away. The music faded into nothingness. Time to move. Time to make his blind way back to the hotel, find out if it was safe to stay there, and if it was, to rest, to sleep, to let his mind and his body heal.

But if it was not safe?

He would go someplace where it was safe.

Simple.

He walked back into the alley, then onto another dark street. He stopped and looked both ways. He listened. Then he looked at the sky, as if he could see his compass there, some guiding star that would lead him out of the maze of Santa Fe to El Rincon.

He had no idea where he was, but he knew he could not be more than a few blocks from the hotel. He didn't know how far he had run, but he could not have run more than a mile or so.

Everything looked different at night. He had no landmarks, since he had only been down a couple of streets between the hotel and the cantina. There was a street sign on one of the corner buildings at the next street. He skulked across the street and stared up at it.

Delgado Street.

Where in hell was Delgado Street? He had no map, and even if he had, he would not know one street from another. Mariposa was the only one he had seen. He felt more at home in the woods, where he could follow paths, find creeks, study moss at the base of trees. Santa Fe was a labyrinth, and all the buildings looked the same at night. All the streets looked the same. All were dark, forbidding.

Left or right? Turn around or go ahead? He saw no lights, heard no sounds. Had he run that far? Away from all the cantinas, all the hotels, all life?

Delgado ran into Esperanza and Esperanza took him to Caridad, and he knew he was lost by the time he reached a street named Iglesia. Church Street. Had he seen any churches? He could not remember any, but he had not been looking for a church. Still, the street name told him something. Something important.

He had wandered away from the dens of iniquity. He was in a quiet part of town, well away from the hustle and bustle of downtown Santa Fe. Now he knew which way to go, because he had been angling left, east perhaps, or north.

Lew turned right and stole through the streets like a thief in the night. He was furtive. He felt like a hunted animal on the prowl, and there was a feeling of safety in that notion, a feeling that he was safe as long as he could not be seen. He began to think of himself as just another animal, but he had not decided on which kind.

Was he a deer making its way through thick trees to the hardwoods where it could feed on fallen acorns? Or a coon slipping down to the creek for a drink of water and perhaps a fish it could catch.

No, he was a cat, a bobcat perhaps, padding quiet over hard ground, stopping every so often to listen, to sniff the air, to explore with all its senses as it hunted for the unwary rabbit or the field mouse, someone's house cat, or a small dog. He walked close to the silent buildings and took his time, staying to the shadows, crossing each street with caution, looking, listening.

He saw a dim light down the way on one of the nameless streets, a spray of golden light pouring from a window. He glided toward it like a bobcat, a shadow moving through shadows.

There it was, the hotel where he and Marylynn had stayed, where she still was, he assumed. A flood of relief came over him. There were the stables, dark and quiet, across the street.

Lew knew where he was.

He had a long walk ahead of him, but at least he knew which way to go. He crept away from El Palacio and headed toward his own hotel. He wondered if she was up in her room, sleeping perhaps, or reading. Maybe pining for him. He shook off those lethal thoughts and kept to the shadowy streets, heading for El Rincon.

He came in the back way, to the barn where Ruben was. He didn't go inside, but waited, watching the back door of the hotel for ten minutes. Then he waited another five minutes before walking across the open space to the door. He let himself inside. He took out his key and opened his door very slowly. He stood to one side, waiting, listening, hoping no one was in his room.

He waited for several seconds, then slipped quickly inside. He closed the door, latched it. He did not light a lamp, but let his eyes become accustomed to the deeper darkness inside. He listened for any scrap of sound.

There was a soft rustle over where his bed stood.

Lew's senses screamed a silent alarm in his brain.

His hand floated down to the butt of his pistol.

"Lew, is that you?"

He heard a click and knew there was a hammer being cocked.

He hunched over and slid his pistol from its holster, silent as a cat.

"Marylynn?" he said.

"It is you. Yes, it's me."

"You've got a gun pointed at me?"

He heard the slide of metal against metal as she eased the hammer down.

"Not anymore," she said. "I'll light the lamp."

"No," he said, "don't light it. I'll come to you."

His voice was a whisper, but it sounded loud to him in the darkness. He slid his pistol back in its holster and fumbled his way to the bed. He reached out, and she grabbed his hands. He eased onto the bed. She was sitting up and she put her arms around him.

Gave him a hug.

At first he wanted to draw away, but her touch felt good. He smelled her. Her hair was scented, and he drew in the perfume as she lay her head on his shoulder, brushed his face with her flowing locks.

"I was worried about you," she said.

"How did you get in here?"

"I told the clerk I was Mrs. Jones, and he let me in. I told him it was a surprise and told him not to say anything. I gave him a silver dollar."

"You rascal," he breathed.

"Where have you been?" she asked.

"Out walking."

He felt her stiffen as she touched the side of his face. Then her hand went down to his side, through the torn shirt, and he felt her fingers touch the sliced skin, the clotted blood.

"Lew, you're hurt," she said. "You've been in a fight."

"I'm not hurt and I didn't get into a fight," he said.

"I need to look at those wounds."

"They're not wounds, Marylynn. Scratches."

"From a knife," she said, as if she knew everything.

"No. Glass."

"Glass?"

"It's a long story."

"Why can't I light a lamp?"

"That's an even longer story. Just sit and be quiet. I'll tell you all about it tomorrow. In the morning."

"I can't wait that long."

"Shhh," he said.

And then he drew her to him and kissed her. She melted in his arms, flowed into them like something supple and willing, and her mouth was warm and wet and set his blood to tingling. He felt himself slipping off the bed and put his hand down to stop himself. He felt something. Something hard and cold and heavy. Metal.

"You trade in that Colt?" he said.

"Yes," she breathed against his face. "I did everything you told me to do."

"Except stay away," he said, and his voice was without rancor or threat, so soft it sounded almost like a prayer, almost like gratitude. And the moon sprayed gauzy light through the window and glazed her soft hair so that it shone with a silvery luster like one of those night paintings of horses by Frederick Remington he had seen in *Harper's Weekly* one day so long ago.

"I stayed away," she whispered.

He started to say something about lying, but she touched her fingers to his lips. She wasn't finished.

"As long as I could," she said.

20

WAYNE MCGARRITY SMITH TRUSTED NO MAN. BUT HIS FATHER, Liam Elmore Smith, who had taught his son everything Wayne valued, had told him he must choose wisely those men who could aid him in quest for the "Holy Grail."

"You delegate those men who will willingly do your bidding, Wayne," his father once said, "and the others you command or rule by putting the fear of the devil in them. You can't be God, but you can be the devil easily enough. Lord knows you come by the ability through your terrible bloodlines, lad."

Wayne smiled every time he thought of his father, and of his mother, too, for that matter. They were a wicked pair, he liked to say, his father from Limerick, Ireland, his mother Scots-bred, but born in Ireland, too, and named Colleen Brook by her parents of the Campbell clan—both cut from the same bolt of cloth.

He rode into Santa Fe with that delegated man, Earl Crisp, and one other, Reed Danvers, one of those who feared him and therefore revered him. Hand-picked men, both tough as hickory nuts, and both obedient to a fault. And obedient, bless their damned souls, only to him.

"You got a place to go, Wayne?" Crisp asked, his face made

raw by the setting sun. The light flickered in his windburned face, softened the contours of his jawline, his hooked nose and the ledge of his brow jutting over squinted pale blue eyes.

"I do, Earl," Smith replied. He never gave any of his men any more information than they needed at any particular point in time.

"Good place?"

"It'll suit us. Won't be there long, but we need to convert all the silver to cash and make ready for my next move."

"You sure do know how to do it, Wayne," Danvers said. "I mean we had fresh horses all the way. That posse's probably still way back in P-yeblo."

Crisp laughed a dry laugh. He licked parched lips.

"They never had a chance," he said.

"Well, we'll see what the other boys did for us. They been here a couple of days. Can't beat that telegraph."

"I forgot about that," Crisp said.

"I didn't," Smith said, sunlight dancing on his sharp features, glinting off his rusty hair, sparking the red bristles of his two-day beard. He looked like a man who had been sculpted out of iron with an ax blade, all lean muscle, no fat, and piercing blue eyes that bored right through a man when his blood was up.

Smith's father had given him good advice when he was a strapping lad just out of school.

"Only fools work for a living, Wayne. The smart man enjoys the profits of other men's labors. You don't need any more schoolin' than you've had. I'll provide the rest."

And, he had, too. Wayne's father was a constable and he had worked as a prison guard before that. What he had learned from criminals would fill an encyclopedia. He passed along much of that information to his son.

"When a crook wants to make a big haul, get a lot of money, light his cigars with dollar bills, you know where he goes, Wayne, my boy?"

"I don't reckon."

"He gets himself in trouble with the law and goes to jail. That's his school. That's where he plans everything and finds the men he needs to carry out the job. In prison, yes siree, sir."

"I don't reckon I would want to spend time in jail. Prison, either, Pa."

"Smart boy, you are, Wayne. Nor was I suggesting it, mind you. You do like me, that's all. You become an officer of the law. That way you get to know criminals, find out their secrets. Ah, yes, that's the beauty of it, don't you see? You befriend the criminals you need and plan your jobs. They carry the jobs out and you're still sitting on your side of the fence."

"Is that what you do, Pa?"

"You don't see us livin' in squalor, do you, Wayne? Do you lack for anything your heart desires? Do you have food on your table, a warm bed to lie in at night? Do you see your dear old mother slavin' like a potato picker in the fields all day? She has a woman to do her washin' and cleanin' and she can read the magazines and make herself pretty every night for her dear sweet husband."

"It doesn't sound hard, anyways. Not if you do it, Pa."

"It ain't hard at all, at all. I'll show you everything I know. You'll be a grand success like your old man. Anyways, if you look at it a certain way, it's all one bunch, criminals and lawfolk."

"What do you mean, Pa?"

"The way I see it, Wayne, it's like when you were a little kid. You and a bunch of kids go out in the play yard and you play coppers and robbers. You choose up sides. All the same bunch, but you take turns playin' first one side, then the other."

And his father had been right. Criminals and lawmen were all of the same ilk, in Wayne's eyes. It just meant you chose one side or the other. You both played the same game. That's how he had made money in Bolivar, and how he was making money now. He was on the side of the law and the men who worked for him carried out his orders. If anything went wrong, they went to jail. He was the man with the badge. Or used to be. Somewhere, not long ago, he had crossed the line.

And so had his father, who was doing time in the penitentiary in Texas, down in Huntsville. But his father was a philosopher and did not take it hard.

"When I get out, Wayne, I'll have a plan that will make my retiring years golden, you'll see. I'm living with the real professionals now, and what I've learned will make me rich. All they have is brawn, boyo. It's your old man who has the brains."

His father had taught him that a life of crime was really the way rich people lived.

"You can work hard all your life, get callouses on your hands, break your back, ruin your health, if you follow the straight and narrow," his father said. "And you'll always be poor and you'll wind up poor.

"Look, son, they teach you honesty in school and that's the way the rich keep the poor underfoot. The most honest man on earth will turn dishonest in a flash if the price is right."

"What do you mean, Pa?"

"I mean the way to the big money is to pay the people who handle it to give it to you without putting a gun to their heads. You take tellers who work in a bank—they handle all that money, day after day, and none of it is theirs. None of it will ever be theirs. But you come along and you offer them a cut if they will let you inside the bank, into the vault where you can take the money. You give them some of the money and they feel as if they've done no wrong. Crime pays, Wayne, because honest people turn dishonest once they realize their greed can be satisfied."

"It sounds so easy, the way you put it, Pa."

"Son, get a job on the police force. You'll soon see how the criminal justice system works."

"How does it work?"

"Money makes it work. The judge, the prosecutor, the sheriff, down to the jailer, all make money off criminals."

"How?"

"I've heard lawyers ask their guilty clients how much time in prison they want to serve. If the man says a year, his defense will cost so much money. That money is divided up among the judge, prosecutor, sheriff, jailer, and so on. If the guilty party does not want to do any jail time, the price goes up. And burglars always get low bail or no bail—that's right off the old ball bat."

"Why?"

"Because burglars can only pay their way if they are burgling, you see. So the lawyer tells the judge, 'This man is a good burglar, your honor. He can bring in five hundred dollars a week and he'll give us half.' So the judge sets bail, and the burglar goes back to work. When he goes to trial, whatever amount he pays his lawyer will tell the judge how long a sentence to order. Slick as a willow whistle, eh?"

And Wayne had found out that this was the way things worked. He had talked to an inside man who worked for Horace Tabor, found out about the silver, and now he was the richer for it. The inside man had little risk if he kept his mouth shut.

They could see the Sangre de Cristo range, with its snow-capped peaks, all purple and hazy in the sunset, rising majestically above the mighty Rio Grande del Norte, the sun banking behind them, shooting golden rays into the long battings of clouds that hung in the sky like rolled-up ropes of cotton.

"When we get settled, Reed, you go fetch Moon and bring him to the hotel. I want to talk to him first. Then, we'll send for the others, lay out all the silver bars, and use them for mirrors while we shave."

"I can hardly wait," Reed said.

Wayne smiled. They were like children, sometimes, his boys. Reed looked like he was strained through a sheet, a thin rail of a man with skin stretched tight over his Adam's apple so that it looked like it would break through, a slender pipe of a nose, small, skinny lips, and hair that grew in every compass direction like an explosion of wheat stalks. But he followed orders and was loyal.

"Do you know the way to this place we're stayin'?" Crisp asked.

"Nope," Wayne said. "Just that it's kinda in the heart of town. I never been here before."

"Me, neither," Crisp said. "Heard a lot about Santa Fe. Supposed to be like a big old trading post."

"There's money to be made here," Wayne said.

"This road ought to go straight to downtown," Crisp said.

"That's what I'm thinkin'," Wayne said, pulling a pack of store-boughts from his pocket. "But just so's you both know, we're stayin' at the Posado del Rio. Friend of mine said it's a right fancy place."

"Anything'd be better'n Pueblo," Crisp said, as Wayne struck a match and lit his cigarette. He didn't offer a smoke to either Crisp or Danvers.

It wasn't quite full dark when the three men reached the center of Santa Fe. They rode around in circles for another ten or fifteen minutes until Crisp spotted the hotel, about a block off the plaza. It took up a full city block, and there were carriages parked outside, a doorman running in and out of the front doors. Trees and grass grew around low brick walls, and lighted lamps threw a soft orange glaze over the walkway. There were hitch rings along one of the low walls and they tied up their horses there.

"You boys just take a seat in the lobby and I'll get us rooms," Wayne said. "No use in all of us goin' up to the desk and scaring the shit out of the clerk."

Crisp and Danvers laughed.

They both sat in plush overstuffed chairs and looked around at the people passing to and fro. None looked at them in their dusty clothes, their unshined boots, grease-stained hats, spurs that could cut the rug on the floor to ribbons. They laid their saddlebags on the floor next to their chairs and lit cigarettes. Both took pleasure in flicking their ashes into the large glass trays sitting on wrought iron stands. Danvers tapped a brass spittoon with the toe of his boot, and grinned idiotically at the dull tinking sound.

Wayne paid cash for the rooms, three of them on the second floor, all with balconies, according to the clerk.

"Little patios with chairs and tables," the clerk said. "A good view of the city from those rooms. Will there be anything else?"

"Send up a bottle of whiskey and a bill of fare," Wayne said. "I see you got a café here." He said the word "café" like he would say "cave." No accent.

"Yes, we have a very fine restaurant here. Open until eleven p.m. I'll see that you have three menus, sir."

He wrote out a receipt and handed it to Smith.

"Now, if you wish, you may sign the register for all three of you," the clerk said, pushing the ledger toward him and pointing to an inkwell sunk in the counter with a fancy pen sticking out of it.

Wayne signed three false names, James Brown, William Jones, and Harry Johnson. The clerk never gave the signatures a second glance and closed the book.

Upstairs in Wayne's room, he spoke to Danvers.

"Reed, you go on to the Tecolote and tell Moon to get his ass over here. Then, you wait an hour and bring anybody else who's there over here."

"What for?" Danvers asked.

"I have to know what's going on—whether there's been any trouble here and if the other boys got down with the silver out of Denver."

"You mean Baker and Riley?"

"Yeah. Them two. Charley Grimes ought to be there, too. And maybe he knows why Cal, Fritz, and Billy never hooked up with us when they was supposed to."

"I wondered about that, too," Crisp said. "We had to pack all that silver by ourselves, 'cept for what Kip and Jethro brung."

"Don't you drink too much now, Reed. We'll eat when the whole bunch is here and have some of the whiskey I got coming up here."

Crisp licked dry lips.

"I'll do her, Wayne," Danvers said. They had lugged their swollen saddlebags up to Wayne's room. He looked at the bags of silver one last time and left the room.

Wayne sat down on the divan and took off his hat.

"Where's that whiskey?" he said to no one.

"Want me to go get it?" Crisp said.

"Naw, we'll wait. Got to have whiskey after a ride like we had."

Crisp grinned.

"You know what, Crisp? Not havin' any whiskey in a room like this is like a bird with one wing."

"Ain't that what the Irish say, Wayne?"

"Yeah, that's what the Irish say, and they're the wisest folk on this green earth."

The two men lit cigarettes. They smoked and waited, until they heard a knock on the door. Crisp opened it.

The whiskey had arrived.

21

BLACKHAWK HAD SOME DIFFICULTY FINDING THE U.S. MAR-
shal's office in Santa Fe. He learned from the head of the
local constabulary that Marshal Cordwainer Vogel had recently moved his office from the police station in the old
presidio to a small street off the main square in downtown
Santa Fe.

"Used to be a military post," Constable Rudolfo Aguilar
explained. "It was empty, and Cord wanted a place to work
that wasn't so busy."

"Yeah, Cord's a loner. That's why they stuck him way out
here in Santa Fe," Blackhawk said. Aguilar gave him directions to the office, and Blackhawk rode there in late afternoon after having lunch in a nondescript Mexican café
called Lupe's, in the shadow of the old fort where so much
of Santa Fe's history had been written.

The office was on Calle Alameda, where there were trees,
cobblestoned streets, a small square or plaza with a number
of other business establishments, and attorneys', assayers',
and land offices. He had to tie his horse outside the com-
pound and walk into the alameda. Typical of Cord Vogel, he
thought, make it real hard to see him.

He hadn't seen Vogel in years, but he knew Cord was a

good man. They had worked half a dozen cases together and Blackhawk knew him to be a dedicated, honest, hardworking lawman. If there was any criticism of the man, it was his elusiveness. He tended to go off on his own hook without checking in with his superiors. But, as that type of individual, Vogel was a man after Blackhawk's own heart.

He entered the modest office, which had a small sign on the outside door that simply read U.S. MARSHAL. A small flag stood on a tall flagpole. A person could get a crook in his neck if he looked up at it for more than a moment.

He approached the desk, behind which sat a young Mexican woman with long black hair drawn up in a bun, an immaculate bronze complexion, lively brown eyes, and a patrician nose. She wore a plain white blouse and looked very efficient. She was busy with stacks of papers arranged in neat piles. There was an In Box and an Out Box on one corner of the desk, and a metal spindle on which were impaled three or four telegraph messages. On one wall there was a corkboard with Wanted posters tacked to it. One of the posters bore the name of Lew Wetzel Zane.

"May I help you?" the woman asked.

"I'm Horatio Blackhawk, U.S. marshal out of Springfield, Missouri. Here to see Marshal Vogel."

"Oh, yes, Mr. Blackhawk, Mr. Vogel said you'd be showing up here. He—he's not here, but he left a letter for you. Let's see, I think it's in this drawer of my desk."

While the woman opened the drawer, Blackhawk sniffed her perfume. Lilacs, he thought, or organdy. She had a touch of rouge on each cheek, none on her lips.

"Where is Cord?" he asked.

She pulled an envelope from the drawer and handed it across the desk.

"He rode off to Socorro yesterday. Said he'd be back inside of a week."

"Socorro? What's going on down there?"

"Murder, I think. Or murders. Including the sheriff. He said he had to investigate."

"Well, I hope to see him while I'm here. Is that all you have for me?"

"Yes. Mr. Vogel doesn't discuss his cases with me. He said to give you the letter."

"All right. Thanks."

There were two benches in the front of the office. Blackhawk sat on one of them and opened the unsealed envelope. He pulled out a single sheet of paper and began to read. He knew Vogel to be an economist with his speech, and he was no less of one with this missive. But at least he had printed it out with block letters so that it was easy to read.

MAN AND WOMAN CHECKED INTO EL PALACIO HOTEL.

MAN SIGNED AS ED JONES.

MAN LEFT NEXT DAY.

WOMAN LEFT FOLLOWING DAY.

JONES STAYED AT EL RINCON.

WOMAN VANISHED. SO DID MAN.

SEE YOU NEXT WEEK.

     CORD.

He turned the paper over, and Cord had listed some names and addresses of the El Palacio and El Rincon hotels, the El Caballero stables, and the name of the owner. Also, cryptically, Cord had written down the name of a cantina without giving any reason why. The name he wrote was the Tecolote, and it was written in script, not block letters, as if it was a hurried afterthought.

"Does that tell you what you want to know?" the woman said to Blackhawk as he put the letter back in the envelope, folded it in half, and stuffed it in his back pocket.

"Just enough to keep me busy. Thanks. I didn't catch your name, ma'am."

"I am Julia Delmonte, sir."

"Pleased to meet you. I'll stop back by in a few days."

"A pleasure," she said politely, then returned to her work.

Blackhawk walked across the alameda, untied his horse, and stepped into the saddle. He'd have to backtrack, find out what happened to Lew Zane and the girl, whose name he had learned was Marylynn Baxter. Cord hadn't said a word about Wayne Smith, but Blackhawk would lay odds that Smith was also in Santa Fe, planning his next robbery.

Alonzo Gutierrez was very helpful, Blackhawk thought. He found him at the Caballero stables after learning that he also owned the hotel across the street, El Palacio.

"The girl, she came in and asked me where she might sell her horse. I told her, and she rode out. She never come back. And when I looked, she had checked out of the hotel. That is all I know."

"Where did you tell her to go?" Blackhawk asked.

"I sent her to the stockyards, where they have the auctions every Thursday. That is tomorrow. So you may find her there."

"What about the man who first rode in with her? Do you know where he is?"

"He leave the next day after they come in. I don't see him no more. And the lady, she does not ask about him."

"He say where he was going, Alonzo?"

"He don't tell me nothing, that man. He just saddle his horse and he ride away. I never see him again. Are these two banditos?"

Blackhawk shook his head and chuckled.

"No. I just need to talk to them. Thanks, Alonzo."

"You are very welcome, Marshal."

He rode to El Rincon and met with the day clerk there, a man named Ralph Sinclair, who said the owner lived in Taos and that he was the manager. Blackhawk asked to see the ledger, and Sinclair showed it to him.

"This man, Ed Jones. He still here?"

"Nope. Left yesterday, with nary a 'by your leave.' Just threw the key on the counter, walked out the back to the barn, and that was that."

"He have a woman with him? A young gal?"

Sinclair shook his head.

"Nope, not that I know of. We don't watch our guests real close."

Blackhawk studied the ledger. He ran a finger over three names that looked suspicious to him.

"What about these three? What do you know about them?"

Sinclair looked at the ledger, scratched his head. He wore a striped shirt, suspenders, and a string tie. He was very neatly dressed, and sported a small handlebar moustache and neatly trimmed sideburns. He looked like a gambler with two garter belts on his sleeves, but Blackhawk knew, from a long study of men, that Sinclair had never played a hand of poker and would surely lose his shirt if he did.

"Those men are still here. They aren't here much, though. They go out every night. To the Tecolote, I think. From the night clerk I gather they stay pretty much there until closing. They don't make much noise. Once in a while some loud talking, but then it's like they whisper."

"What kind of men do you take them for, Mr. Sinclair?" Blackhawk asked.

"Hmm, now let me see. They don't seem like regular businessmen. I don't think cattle. Or sheep. I guess they're just traveling men. Night clerk said they came in all dusty and unshaved. Now they look pretty decent. In a rough sort of way, I guess."

Blackhawk pulled a flyer from his pocket, unfolded it, lay it on the counter.

"Does this drawing look like anybody who's stayed here in the past week?"

Sinclair bent over and examined the likeness on the flyer. He stood up straight and shook his head.

"Nope. Don't recognize him as anybody who's stayed here."

"You got a lead pencil, a piece of charcoal?" Blackhawk asked.

Sinclair opened a drawer, took out a stub of a pencil, handed it to Blackhawk. The marshal began drawing a beard over the chin of Zane's likeness. Then he turned the flyer around and told Sinclair to look at it again.

"Why, now that I see it, maybe. Does resemble that man Jones. Only Jones has a lot more beard than that."

"Thanks, Mr. Sinclair. Now, do you have any idea where Jones might have gone?"

"He didn't ask me or anyone who works here about another hotel. Maybe he left town."

"Yes, maybe he did," Blackhawk said. "Those other men whose names are here in your book, are they in?"

"Why, yes, I believe they are. Do you want their room numbers?"

"I'll take them, but don't you tell them I was asking after them, hear?"

Sinclair shook his head.

"No, sir, I surely will not. Are they . . . ?"

"Don't you fret about it none, Mr. Sinclair. I was just curious, that's all. Where do they board their horses?"

"We have a small barn out back. Mr. Jones kept his horse there. But, of course, it's gone now, and so is he."

"Thank you." Blackhawk left, rode around to the alley and to the back of the hotel. He tied his horse out of sight and walked to the small barn. He looked over the horses, studied their brands. Then, he looked at their hooves, the marks they made on the ground.

He didn't recognize any of them, nor their hoofprints. But he knew Smith and his bunch had switched horses several times. He didn't know if the three men in the hotel had any connection to Wayne, but Sinclair had mentioned that same name that was scrawled on the back of Cord's note. Tecolote. That could be where he might find Smith and the others who had helped him rob Horace Tabor in Denver.

He left and rode back to El Palacio, where he took a room and boarded his horse. He ate supper in the dining room that night and then rode into town, looking for the Tecolote.

He didn't expect to run into Wayne Smith there. Smith wouldn't be that easy to find. But he wanted to look the place over, see if he could spot the hard cases who were staying at El Rincon. At the very least he wanted to see what kind of a place it was and why Cord had scrawled the name on the back of his note.

When he got to the Tecolote, he saw the three horses tied up out front that had been in the barn behind El Rincon. So, the three using fictitious names were inside. He looked at the other horses, too, checked their brands.

There was one that he recognized. He drew back in surprise.

The horse belonged to a man who had been with Smith in
Pueblo. Blackhawk suspected the man was involved in the
Tabor robbery. The man was wanted in three states for murder, bank robbery, and stagecoach theft, along with other as-
sorted crimes, going back to when he was a kid in Kansas.
He knew the man, knew what he looked like, and knew
he worked for Wayne Smith. He knew him from dozens of
posters, flyers, and from seeing him in the Springfield jail
once. He had escaped and was still on the loose. Oh, yes, he
knew this man, what he looked like and what he did.

He just hoped the man didn't know him by sight.

The man's name was Freddie Moon.

22

THE PRIMAVERA HOTEL ON AVENIDA JUAREZ WAS SMALL, NON-descript, out of the way. Which was why Lew had chosen it for him and Marylynn. This was not a street lined with beggars, like so many of the more commercial ones. There were a few *tiendas*, little shops proclaiming *abarrotes* and *panaderia*, a *farmacia*, and various other poor adobes that sold everything from food to clay pots and ashtrays.

"This is more like a boardinghouse than a hotel," Marylynn said after they had settled in their room. "Did you see the little dining hall?"

"Yes. Reasonable, too."

"You mean cheap."

"Yeah, cheap. Main thing is we're away from the main part of town. It's quiet here. If a bunch of hard cases rode up the street, the people would set up a hue and cry. We'd be warned."

"What are you going to do next? I hope you're not . . ."

"Tomorrow, we'll trade horses at the auction," he said. "You need to get a small horse, fourteen or fifteen hands high. You're just a tiny thing."

"Tiny?"

"Well, small, for a woman."

"You don't like small women?"

"Marylynn, don't start an argument over nothing. You're here only because I felt sorry for you. Don't get used to it."

"No argument. But you keep bringing up unpleasant subjects, Lew. You just can't wait to get rid of me, can you?"

"I wouldn't say that."

"Well, I would."

She touched the tabletop, saw that it had been dusted and didn't need something done to it. She had gone over the entire room, small as it was, looking for something to clean. The truth was, the room was spick-and-span, neat as the proverbial pin. She felt useless, as unwanted as dirty soapsuds.

"Marylynn, come sit down," Lew said. "We've got to talk this out right here and now."

She bowed her head and sat down, like an obedient child. But her eyes were flashing with hope. Lew sat on the other chair, a small table between them. She looked up at him, batted her eyelashes.

"Yes?" she said, with a look of longing in her eyes, eyes that bored straight into his with a fixed, searching stare.

Lew cleared his throat, tried not to look at her.

"Damn, this is hard," he said.

"What?" she asked innocently.

"What I have to say, Marylynn."

"Don't say it, then."

"I have to say it. You don't know."

"Don't know what?"

"What you're getting into with me."

"I know. You're a wanted man."

"That's only half of it," he said.

"Half of it? What's the other half?"

He knew she was being coy, teasing him. She was a lot smarter than her imbecilic questions. He knew that. He drew in a breath, looked out the window. There was a flower box there, just outside, blooming with red and yellow flowers, a splash of color in a drab world of adobe brick. A fly buzzed in the room, an irritating fugue to the silence between them.

He put his hands down flat on the table, splayed his fingers into spiky, fleshy fans. He looked down at them, his brow knitting, furrows running across his forehead and the bridge of his nose.

"Four men tried to kill me the other night. I expect Marshal Blackhawk to show up any day now. He's the one chasing me all the way from Missouri."

"I know. You told me."

"These other men. I think they're part of a kind of gang, here to meet up with a bad man I had a run-in with in Pueblo."

"You didn't tell me about him."

"No, because that was a part of my life you sure didn't need to know."

"I'm interested in everything about you, Lew. You know that."

"Stop it, Marylynn. This isn't sweet talk." He felt the anger boil up in him, not at her so much as at himself, for even talking to her like this.

"I didn't mean anything," she said. "Go on. Who is this man and what happened in Pueblo?"

"This man is from Missouri, too. His name is Wayne Smith. He took out an insurance policy on his wife, Carol. They had two little kids. Wayne murdered her so he could collect the money when she was dead."

"How awful."

"I saw him do it. Well, I mean I saw him right after he did it. He killed his kids, too."

Marylynn stiffened, rocked backward in her chair, a look of shock on her face.

"Why, that's terrible," she said. "You tried to catch him."

"Yes, but that's not the important part. Wayne had abandoned her, up in Leadville. Left her and her children to fend for themselves or starve. I met her up there."

He stopped and closed his fingers, slid his hands toward himself, gripped the edge of the table. He felt Marylynn's eyes on him. The fly buzzed past his nose and he swatted at it. Sunlight streamed through the flowers and into the room. The flowers glowed like sunlit stained glass, their petals like the gossamer wings of butterflies, delicate, quivering in a light breeze that wafted past the window.

"What is it, Lew? What happened didn't have anything to do with you, did it? I mean, you couldn't have stopped it, could you?"

"No. I helped the woman out. She was a nice lady."

A sadness crept into his voice. Marylynn cocked her head and stared at him in puzzlement.

"There's more to it, isn't there?" she said.

"Yes."

"What is it, Lew?"

"I loved her," he said. "We were going to get married. She was going to divorce Wayne. She never got the chance."

"Oh, I'm so sorry, Lew. I didn't know."

The silence again. The buzzing fly. The flowers in the window box dulling now as a cloud passed over the sun and the breeze died. There was a somnolence to the moment.

Lew sighed as the silence turned awkward.

"I'm sorry, too," he said. "This Wayne Smith—I think he's here in Santa Fe. Some of his men are here. They're the ones who tried to kill me the other night."

"Because of you and Carol?"

"No. I don't know if they know about that. Maybe Wayne does. I don't know. No, I think it's that reward. A man named Grimes. I met him in Las Vegas at the hotel there. He picked up that flyer in Glorieta, you know."

"Yes. You mentioned him. Charley Grimes."

"So, I've got those men trying to put lead in me, and Blackhawk on my trail. That's why you have to go out on your own. Stay away from me."

"But I could help you, Lew. I bought that pistol. I carry it all the time."

He shook his head.

"No, you can't help. They'd kill you and never even bat an eye."

"I'm not afraid of them."

"I am. For you. Now, I've told you why you have to forget about me. I have to go through this alone, Marylynn. Please don't get in my way."

"I won't. But that doesn't mean I have to leave you. I'll wait for you. Until it's all over and you come back."

He gave her a wry smile.

"You're a hard head, you know that?"

"That's what my daddy always said. He said I had grit."

"You got more than grit, Marylynn. You got a bad case of foolishness."

"Oh, pshaw, Lew. You say the sweetest things."

"Don't," he said. "Don't make it any worse than it is. Now, tonight, I'm going out. I may not come back. If I don't, you make your way in the world and forget you ever met me."

"You know I can't do that," she said.

He got up from the table.

"Suit yourself. Just don't follow me tonight. Promise?"

She hesitated.

"Promise," he ordered.

"I promise," she said, crossing one of her fingers in the hand that was in her lap. "I'll stay right here."

When the sun started to go down, he strapped on his gunbelt, kissed Marylynn, and then was gone. He warned her one more time to stay there and told her that he would be back.

But he wondered if he would return. He had to find out where Wayne Smith was, if he could. And to do that, he had to keep an eye on the Tecolote. He wouldn't go in, but he'd see who came and went and follow any one of those four men who looked as if he were meeting up with Smith.

It was a long shot, but it was the only one he had.

Half an hour later, Lew tied his horse to a hitch rail one block away from the Tecolote. The sky had blazed for a long time behind the Sangre de Cristo range and was now dark as pitchblende, sprinkled with uncountable stars, the Milky Way a broad band of diamond dust and Venus winking brighter than any of them just above the horizon.

Lew walked to the next street, where he could see the Tecolote and its glowing lamps. He stood in a dark shadow in the doorway of an adobe shop that sold Hopi and Navajo pottery, blankets, dolls, and trinkets. The front window was dusty and cast no reflection when he passed it and took up his position.

He waited an hour, studying every man who entered or left the cantina. Finally, he saw Moon ride up and dismount. He came from the direction of the town center. Half an hour later, he saw Grimes ride in from another direction. Grimes dismounted and looked hard up and down the street. Lew stood stock-still and held his breath. Then, Grimes entered the saloon.

Twenty minutes later, from the direction of El Rincon Hotel, Lew saw Baker, riding up at a brisk canter. Baker didn't look around as Grimes had done, but tied up his horse and strode into the cantina as though he was in a hurry.

Lew relaxed. He knew he might have to wait there all night before any of the four men left.

He felt the evening chill come on and leaned against the adobe wall and the heavy door.

Voices drifted from the cantina and he heard the clink of glasses. Other men came up and went inside, but none that he knew.

Then, he heard the scrape of a boot and stiffened at the sound. It had come from his left, several yards away. If he leaned out he could see who was coming, but he would give his position away.

His right hand floated downward, hovered over the butt of his pistol like a silent hawk holding to the wind.

Silence.

Then, a moment later, a crunching sound as if the person approaching had taken another step.

Lew's fingers closed around the Colt's grip.

Crunch. Scrape.

He eased the pistol from its holster, rested his thumb on the hammer.

"Don't draw that Colt, Zane," said a voice so close, it sent a shiver of electricity through Lew's body.

He knew the voice.

He didn't draw his pistol, but he eased it farther out of the holster and rubbed the hammer with his thumb.

He waited.

23

ANOTHER CRUNCH OF GRAVEL UNDERFOOT, AND HORATIO Blackhawk loomed up out of the shadow, two feet from where Lew stood, his right hand gripping the butt of his Colt.

"Evenin', Lew," Blackhawk said.

Lew saw that the marshal wasn't holding a pistol in his hand.

"Mr. Blackhawk."

"You won't need that pistol just yet, Lew. I'm not here to arrest you."

Lew didn't move.

"Unless you're going to shoot me," Blackhawk said.

Lew couldn't see Blackhawk's face well, but an image of him smiling flashed in Lew's mind. He released his grip on the pistol and drew in a breath as he relaxed.

"No," Lew said. "But . . ."

"I saw your horse. Fact is, I saw you ride up. I tied mine right next to yours."

"But how . . . ?"

"I figured you were going to keep an eye on that cantina over there. Sure enough, here you are. Seems like we both got the same idea."

"I don't know what you're talking about, Mr. Black-hawk."

"Why don't you call me Horatio, Lew? Forget the mister."

"All right. I still don't know . . ."

"Wayne Smith," Blackhawk said.

Lew stiffened at the mention of the name.

"He got away, then," Lew said.

"Pretty dadgummed slick, you ask me," Blackhawk said. "Pulled off a robbery in Denver, got clean away. Tracked him to right here in Santa Fe."

"You've seen him?"

Blackhawk moved into the doorway with Lew, stood less than a foot from him. Now Lew could see his face from the dim light of the cantina. He was clean-shaven and smelled of lye soap and the faintest aroma of rosewater, as if he had been to a barber.

"No, but he's here."

"How come you're not arresting me?" Lew asked.

"I figure you and I have a mutual interest in Wayne Smith. I want him. I want him bad. Maybe as bad as you do."

"His men, some of them, anyway, are inside that cantina right now."

"You know who they are? That's information I could use. Might buy you a little more freedom, Zane."

"How much freedom?"

"Let's just say I've got my hands full trying to catch Smith."

"He's more important to you than I am," Lew said.

"At the moment, yes."

"All right."

Lew told him the names of the men inside the Tecolote, without elaborating on any of them.

"That fits," Blackhawk said. "I've spent a lot of the day tracking Freddie Moon, checking on him, and I'm beginning to put together a picture of what's going on here in Santa Fe. I think I know why Smith came here. And who he's going to rob. But I still need to find him."

"Moon just got here the other night, I think," Lew said.

"Yeah, he left for a few days. But for the past six or seven months, he's been working for a big freighter here, and I think I know why."

"But you're not going to tell me," Lew said.

"No. I can't risk it right now. If I ever put it all together, I might fill you in, Lew. Right now, I'm mighty tempted to swear you in as a deputy U.S. marshal."

"Huh?"

Blackhawk grinned.

"But we get many temptations in life, don't we?"

"Why would you even think such an outlandish thing?"

"Because I'm going to ask for your help. Just for a day or two, maybe."

"My help?" Lew reared his head back in surprise.

Two men rode up, dismounted, hitched their horses, and walked inside the Tecolote. Both Lew and Horatio looked at them, and then at each other. Both shook their heads.

"Just a couple of drinking hands," Blackhawk said.

"I don't recognize them, either. But let's get back to what you were saying, Marsh—er, uh, Horatio."

"The way I see it, Smith didn't ride into Santa Fe alone. The men who work for him are all criminals. They either were in jail back in Bolivar where he met them, or were in the prison where Smith's father was a guard. There are a lot of them, and Smith knows how to use them. Those men take most of the chances, so Smith can operate. He's the brains of the outfit."

"You know a lot about him," Lew said.

"Yeah, I do."

"So what do you need me for?"

"The territorial marshal is out of town. The police force here has its hands full. I want to flush Smith out, find out where he is, put him in irons if I can."

"And if you do?"

"He'll first stand trial in Pueblo for the murder of his wife and kids. Then he'll be tried in Denver for the Horace Tabor robbery. After that, I don't know. And I don't care."

"Where do you think he is?" Lew asked.

"He's got a lot of silver with him. I figure he'll convert that to cash, then carry out whatever crime brought him to Santa Fe. And I've got a strong hunch what he'll go after."

"But that's what you don't tell me."

"That information could get you killed, Zane. Real quick like."

"All right. How do you plan to flush Smith out of hiding?"

"I think Freddie Moon is acting kind of like a courier between Smith and those other men inside the Tecolote. You told me he came from town, and that the others are staying at El Rincon."

"Yeah, a couple of them are, at least. I don't know where Grimes fits in, but he's with them, all right. He wants to collect the reward on me, and now he's probably shown that flyer to Smith and the others."

"So you've got a criminal posse chasing after you," Blackhawk said.

"A funny way to put it."

"It amounts to that."

"Yeah, from a lawman's point of view, I reckon it does. It's not funny to me. You're enough posse for me right now, Horatio."

"Look, Lew, I think you're getting the short end of the stick back in Arkansas. But I am sworn to do my duty, so I'm bound to take you back there. However, there's no time limit on when I have to do that. So for now, I'm not a posse on your trail, all right?"

"If you say so, Horatio."

"Look, I think Moon is giving orders to those other men in there. Orders from Wayne Smith. In a little while, he'll be coming out and heading back to where Smith is holed up. I think it will take two of us to follow him. He'll use these streets like a switchback and watch his backtrail. If he sees me following him, he'll turn a corner, go to another street. He could do that all night and I'd never get him to go to Smith."

"He's that smart?"

"He's that smart. But if we both work it right, he'll never catch on."

"Two would be just as obvious as one, seems to me."

"Yeah, if we rode together. I have a different idea."

"I'm listening," Lew said, his glance still on the batwing doors across the street.

In the silence between them, there was only the sound of voices spilling out from the saloon, the switch of a horse's tail, the stomp of a shod foot, or a pawing at the hitch ring, which sounded like someone clanging a horse-shoe against an iron post, and the occasional rise and fall of laughter.

"Say you give Moon a good lead when he leaves here. You run and get your horse, which should give him that much, and you stay on him until he turns a street. I'll be on my horse, back far enough to see you, but too far for him to see me. He turns right, you give me a signal. I ride over to the next street and pick him up. Then, you get behind me and I follow him a ways until he turns again, then we switch."

"It might work," Lew said.

"It's all I can think of. Does Moon know what you look like? Or does he know your horse?"

"I don't think so. Not in the dark. He's probably seen my picture on that flyer. But my beard has grown out, and he'd be hard put to find my face in the dark."

"He doesn't know me, either," Blackhawk said. "But you go on over now and get your horse, ride back here, and tie up down at the far end of the street on the east end. Then I'll bring my horse over and we'll be ready to go."

"I'm game," Lew said.

"I'll be here." Blackhawk moved aside as Lew stepped out from the doorway. Lew walked briskly up the street, turned in at an opening between two buildings, then ran to the next street. He patted Ruben on the neck, unwrapped his reins, and climbed into the saddle. In moments, he was at the east end of the street. He dismounted and waited. He thought he saw Blackhawk slip away, but it was so dark he couldn't be sure. He strained to keep an eye on the Tecolote, then re-alized he wouldn't be able to tell much if anyone came out.

Instead, he fixed his gaze on Moon's horse, which was easier on his eyes.

A few moments later he heard the soft thud of hoofbeats coming down the street behind him. He waited, and when they drew close, he turned and saw Blackhawk riding into view. He turned right and headed for the deep shadows on the opposite side of the street. He probably had a better view of the cantina than Lew did from that vantage point.

The two men waited another fifteen minutes before anyone came out of the Tecolote.

Two men, their arms around each other's shoulders, staggered out onto the street and walked zig-zaggedly down the thoroughfare in the opposite direction. Five minutes later, a lone man emerged and stood to one side of the batwing doors, outside, looking both ways, up and down the street.

Lew leaned against Ruben, patted his chest to keep him quiet. Ruben's ears pricked up and swiveled toward the man outside the Tecolote.

The man stepped away from the saloon and crossed the street.

It was Moon.

Lew held his breath as Moon mounted his horse, glanced Lew's way without seeing him, and then headed west toward the center of town. Just before he got too far away to see, Lew climbed up in his saddle and headed the same way, holding Ruben to a walk.

He didn't look back. He knew Blackhawk would follow when he judged it to be safe. As he rode, he saw Moon, just the barest silhouette of him. He seemed in no hurry, as if he were riding slow just to catch somebody following him.

They rode four blocks like that, Lew keeping the same distance between him and Moon, There was a soft glow in the sky from the lamps lighting the streets in downtown Santa Fe. He passed a few people out walking, a café that was still open, and another cantina called El Coronado, and still Moon held to his steady pace, riding on the right side of the thoroughfare.

Then Moon turned right, two blocks from Lew.

Lew turned and signaled to Blackhawk. He saw him turn right at a gallop and disappear in seconds, heading for the next street.

A beggar emerged from the shadows, holding out his hand. He was wearing rags and a tattered straw hat, sandals on his dirty feet. A streetlamp lit him. Lew turned his horse away and heard the man curse him in Spanish.

He rode one block past where he had seen Moon turn, and then he turned to the right.

Blackhawk rode past at the next intersection, waved at Lew, then continued on. Lew took his time getting to the cross street. When he turned, he rode into light from streetlamps and saw them showing his way on both sides of the street. Two blocks beyond, he caught a glimpse of Blackhawk plodding along, and two blocks behind him, he saw a tiny figure on horseback that must be Freddie Moon.

He kept his eyes on Blackhawk, in case he signaled that Moon had turned again, but five blocks farther on, the streets were brightly lit with gaslight lamps. Their halos swirled with moths and other flying insects. Young men and women strolled the plaza, and some were grouped around a grassy spot with a gazebo in the center. He could smell the aroma of beer and whiskey, saw other young men, bare-chested, sitting on benches, passing bottles back and forth.

People streamed in all directions and, for a moment, Lew lost sight of Blackhawk. He stood up in the saddle, but he could no longer see Moon. He glanced to his right and saw a large hotel with trees planted outside and a canvas awning over a walkway. The sign read POSADO DEL RIO, and there, in front, he saw Moon's horse tied to a hitch ring.

No sign of Blackhawk.

Lew halted Ruben and turned and looked around everywhere.

"He went inside," a voice said.

Lew turned the other way and there was Blackhawk, the merest smirk on his face.

"You scared the hell out of me, Horatio. Sneaking up on a man like that."

"I had to stay out of sight. I was over behind those bushes yonder, in them trees."

Lew saw them, to the far right of the hotel, a small grove, with bushes and what looked like date trees, but could have been box elder. He couldn't tell because all of it was in shadow.

"You saw Moon go in?"

"Not only that, but Wayne Smith was outside, waiting for him. They walked in together."

Lew let out a breath.

"Now what?" he said.

"Now you earn your deputy's pay. I'm going to have to swear you in, Lew."

"We're going in after Smith?"

"Sure as your daddy loved poke," Blackhawk said, and smiled with a grin like a picket fence in the moonlight.

24

LEW LOWERED HIS RIGHT HAND AFTER INTONING THE WORDS, "So help me God."

"You're duly sworn, Zane," Blackhawk said. "Now, let's tie up our horses and get inside that hotel."

"That was a short swearing in, Horatio."

"Yeah, and probably wasn't legal."

"Not legal?"

"No Bible, no flag, no justice of the peace or judge."

"That gives me a lot of comfort."

"It's legal enough. If the local law mixes in, you can tell them you're a deputy U.S. marshal. I'll back you up."

They rode over to some hitch rings along the low brick wall and dismounted. They quickly tied their reins to the rings and started to stride toward the hotel entrance.

Suddenly, they heard the sound of hoofbeats, and both men turned to see three riders galloping toward the hotel, hell bent for leather. Strollers moved out of their way. The riders stopped a few yards from the hotel as the man in the lead held up his hand. Then he dropped his arm slightly and pointed toward Lew.

"There he is, the bastard."

Lew's heart seemed to stop dead in his chest.

It was Charley Grimes, and he was already reaching for his sidearm.

"Duck," Blackhawk said as Grimes drew his pistol and took aim.

Both men dove for the bushes in front of the hotel as the men with Grimes, Baker and Riley, spilled from their horses, their pistols drawn. They swatted the rumps of their horses, and the animals humped up and leapt away at a run.

Grimes fired his pistol as Blackhawk knocked Lew to the ground behind the low wall, into a clump of bushes.

Lew could hear Grimes running toward them, his boots coming down hard on the flange of cobblestones that bordered the front of the hotel. Lew clawed for his pistol as Blackhawk rolled away into the concealing shrubs.

Grimes fired again, and the bullet skidded across a brick, spun off in a caroming whine before it thudded into the heavy outer wall of the hotel. Lew heard a shot from behind him and knew that Blackhawk had drawn a bead on one of the charging men. He raised his head and saw Grimes clutch his belly. But he didn't go down.

He put his left hand over his belly and blood pushed through his fingers, gushing from his gut in a crimson torrent. Grimes staggered forward, hammering back his pistol for another shot. Blackhawk fired again, and the bullet caught Grimes high in the right side of his chest, spinning him offstride. He staggered under the impact and took aim on Blackhawk's position.

Lew lifted his pistol, thumbing the hammer back, and snapped off a shot at Grimes. The bullet slammed into his breastbone. Lew heard it crack like a walnut. Grimes sank to his knees, his eyes rolling wildly in their sockets. He grunted, but did not go down. He looked toward Lew and swung his pistol, taking aim even as he was obviously dying. Lew wasted no time. He squeezed the trigger of his Colt and saw Grimes twitch midway in the swing of his arm. The bullet caught him in the throat. Blood gushed from the wound as if someone had exploded a catsup can, flowing down his neck and soaking his shirt until it looked like the side of an Iowa barn.

Grimes crumpled in a heap, releasing the grip on his pistol. His fingers twitched as the gun hit the ground with a thud, puffing up a tiny cloud of dust.

Baker and Riley split up and tried to flank Blackhawk and Zane. They ran hunched over like sniffing bloodhounds, and they were fast, so fast Lew had trouble tracking them. He heard Blackhawk's pistol roar, and saw his bullet kick up dirt a half yard behind Riley, chipping off a chunk of brick that tumbled through the air like a jerked-out tooth. Riley fired back at Blackhawk and the bullet ripped through small limbs, cracking them like matchsticks, mangling leaves to shreds before it thudded into the hotel wall, scattering painted plaster in all directions.

Baker hesitated, then dashed straight at the edging wall and leaped over it. Blackhawk blasted off a shot, but missed.

"Got to reload, Lew. Can you handle it?"

"Yeah," Lew said, and cracked off a shot at Riley, who had stopped and turned to take aim at Blackhawk. Just as Lew squeezed the trigger, Riley fired and then threw himself headlong onto the ground. He sprawled there and rolled over toward the wall for cover.

Lew's bullet whined off a cobblestone, winging into the starry night. People who had been nearby a few moments before were either huddled against buildings, or had disappeared. It was strangely quiet.

Lew could hear Blackhawk feeding fresh cartridges into the cylinder of his pistol. He heard the slide working to eject the empty hulls. Lew had lost count of how many times he had fired, but knew he would have to reload after another shot or two, unless he was already empty. It was difficult to see Riley, and Baker had vanished into some brush. Lew would not know where Baker was until Baker fired his pistol and Lew could see the flash.

A man walked out of the hotel and stood there for a moment in confusion. He looked at all the people huddled in fear beyond the walkway. He saw a woman run across the plaza and the streaming fountain and knew something was wrong. He turned right around and went back inside the hotel.

"I'm loaded," Blackhawk said, and Lew heard a rustling in the bushes as the marshal changed position.

He took that interval to eject his spent cartridges and reload. He kept his head down, hugged the ground. Riley was no more than thirty feet away and could be preparing to attack.

"See anybody?" Blackhawk asked.

"I just reloaded."

"I'm going after the one who ran into the bushes."

"That's Baker," Lew said and lifted his head to peer over the wall.

That's when Riley rose up and fired his pistol. Lew ducked, but the bullet sizzled past his ear and the hairs rose on the back of Lew's neck as a shiver rippled up his spine. Riley fired again, and Lew heard the bullet spang into the wall, spitting up fragments of brick.

Blackhawk was moving. Lew heard more rustling behind him. Then he saw Baker push aside a branch and take a bead on the marshal.

"Look out, Horatio," Lew gruffed. Then he crawled a few feet on his belly and lifted his head again. Riley had flattened out again, but Lew could see the crown of his hat.

He knew where Riley was. Lew dug his hand into the dirt and picked up a clump. Then he tossed it over the side of the low wall, straight at Riley.

Riley fired off another shot, and that's when Lew stuck his head up and used the wall to brace his pistol. He shot and saw his bullet hit the crown of Riley's hat, tearing it from his head. The hat sailed a few feet, then sank to the ground. Riley fired again just as Lew ducked back down.

Baker fired two quick shots into the bushes behind Lew. He waited to hear a groan from Blackhawk, but none came. Instead, Blackhawk fired off a shot at Baker. Lew heard the bullet splash through leaves and strike a tree trunk with a loud thunk, like a hammer hitting wood.

A man emerged from the hotel's front entrance, carrying a shotgun.

"What the hell's going on out here?" he yelled.

Baker shot him where he stood. The man staggered a few

feet, then dropped to the ground. His shotgun clattered on the stone walk.

Blackhawk fired another shot in the direction of Baker, and Baker returned fire almost immediately.

Lew crawled two more feet and grabbed another handful of dirt. He tossed it where he thought Riley would be and heard the clod hit something. He raised up for a quick glimpse, then ducked his head just before Riley fired.

Lew came up with his Colt and saw Riley looking down at his pistol.

"Drop it, Riley," Lew yelled.

Riley brought his pistol up to bear on Lew. Lew fired from twenty feet away. Riley let out a grunt as the bullet struck him just above the belt buckle. A red stain spread across his shirt and he took aim at Lew. His shot went wild, sizzling over Lew's head.

Lew shot him again, right in the heart.

Riley did a slow pirouette as he sank to the ground. His pistol tumbled from his fingers and clacked on the cobblestones. He sprawled facedown and didn't move.

"You got him, Lew," Blackhawk said, and Lew heard the bushes rustle again as the marshal moved closer to where Baker was hiding.

"Baker, you better give up," Blackhawk yelled. "If you don't want to join Grimes and Riley on Boot Hill."

"You come and get me," Baker said.

"No sooner said than done," Blackhawk said.

Lew rolled over toward some flowers and bushes. He pointed his pistol where he had last seen Baker, looking for any movement, any sign that Baker was going to expose his position.

He couldn't see Blackhawk, nor could he hear him.

A woman whimpered somewhere off toward the plaza and Lew heard the sound of running feet off in the distance as someone ran for cover at a more distant location.

Then the doors to the hotel opened, and another man came out, ducking his head. He looked around, then went back inside. Lew didn't recognize him.

"Damn," Blackhawk said.

"What?" Lew asked.

"That was one of Smith's men who just came out. I recognized him."

A shot rang out from where Baker was hiding, and Lew heard the bullet smack into a tree, shaking it. Some leaves fell to the ground. Then, Blackhawk fired at Baker.

Lew knew he was in a bad spot. Baker hadn't seen him yet, but if he moved a few feet closer, Lew knew that he'd be spotted.

A series of clicks and metal scrapings drew Lew's attention. Baker was reloading. He steeled himself.

"Now or never," he breathed and got to his feet. He jumped the sidewall and ran along it, hunched over. He circled the place where Baker was concealed.

He looked back to see Blackhawk emerge from the bushes. He charged straight at the place where Baker was standing. Lew saw Baker move. He stopped, fired a shot at Baker.

Blackhawk, in a crouch, hurried toward Baker. Baker swung on Lew, then switched to bring his pistol to bear on the marshal.

Too late.

Blackhawk fired, and Baker spun away from the tree. Blackhawk was on top of him in seconds.

"Drop your pistol, Baker," Blackhawk ordered.

"Damn you to hell," Baker snarled.

Blackhawk shot him once in the belly, then again in the chest. Baker groaned in pain, then keeled over, mortally wounded.

Lew ran over to look down at Baker.

"He's done for, Horatio."

"I know. We've got to get in that hotel, find Smith."

Baker let out a last gasp, then lay still, his hand still gripping his pistol.

Lew started toward the hotel entrance. Blackhawk began to trot and passed him. They swept into the lobby.

"Where'd that man go who was just outside?" he asked the startled clerk.

The clerk cocked a thumb toward the rear of the hotel.

"Him and two others went out the back way. You just missed them."

"Stay here, Lew," Blackhawk said, and raced down the hallway, out of sight. Lew heard a door open and then slam shut. He stood by the counter, feeling the clerk's stare on the side of his face.

"Are you robbers?" the clerk asked.

Lew looked at the pistol in his hand. The clerk's hands were raised in a gesture of surrender. Lew holstered the Colt.

"U.S. marshals," he said. "Put your hands down."

"Yes, sir," the clerk said, but he kept his hands dangling chest high.

Blackhawk returned in a few moments.

"They got clean away," he said.

"I want to look in Smith's room," Blackhawk told the clerk.

"We don't have any Smith registered here," the clerk said.

"Those men have three rooms?"

"Yes sir."

"Give me the keys to all three, then."

"I don't . . ."

Blackhawk waved his pistol.

"Yes, sir," the clerk said and turned to the boxes behind him. He threw three keys on the counter and backed off, his hands held shoulder high.

They checked all three rooms. Smith's room was the largest, and that's where they found empty sacks that had once held silver.

Lew reached in his pocket and took out the bar he had been carrying.

"I found this over at El Rincon," he told Blackhawk. "Baker, or one of them, dropped it through a hole in a sack like one of these."

"I think Smith has already converted those bars to cash. And now he's gone. He's got at least two men left. But it's not going to do him any good."

"Why?" Lew asked.

"Because I know what the bastard's got planned. And we'll have time to stop him."

"We?"

"Until Marshal Vogel gets back from Socorro, you're my deputy, Zane. I said 'we.' "

"Horatio, I hate the law. The law ruined my life. I won't help you."

"You will or I'll put you in jail tonight. And throw away the damned key."

Lew looked around the empty room. He was free, but he felt trapped. And Marylynn was waiting for him. She was probably worried.

"How long before Smith makes his move?" Lew asked.

"Thursday's the day," Blackhawk said.

"How do you know that?"

"That's Cinco de Mayo, Lew."

Lew had no idea what Blackhawk was talking about.

25

WAYNE SMITH HAD JUST FINISHED PACKING HIS SADDLEBAGS when there was a knock on his door at the Posado del Rio. He drew his pistol and walked to the door, stood to one side of it.

"Yeah?"

"It's me, Crisp."

Smith holstered his pistol and opened the door.

"Where's Reed?" he asked as Earl Crisp strode through the door lugging his saddlebags and bedroll.

"He's comin', I reckon. He's slower'n turtle shit on a cold day."

"Moon ought to be here any minute," Smith said, closing the door. He dragged his saddlebags across the room and set them by the door.

"What about Charley and them?"

"They're comin', too. We can't stay here no more," Smith said. "Too many people know where I am. We only got two days, maybe, to get everything ready."

"You're set then, Wayne?"

"I'll know by tomorrow. I think so."

Someone was banging on the door.

"That's Reed now, I reckon," Crisp said.

"Well, make damn sure. And if it is, let him in. Then we'll go down to the lobby and wait for Charley Grimes, Baker, and Riley. Horses all saddled and ready to go?"

"Yep," Crisp said. "They're tied up out back, like you said."

"I got a funny feelin'," Smith said as Crisp went to the door.

"That you, Danvers?" Crisp called through the door.

"Who the hell you think it is?" Danvers replied. "Open up, will ya?"

Crisp opened the door, let Danvers inside. He, too, was carrying his saddlebags and bedroll, rifle and sheath.

"What was that you said, Wayne?" Crisp asked after he had closed the door.

"I said I got me a funny feelin' tonight."

"How come?"

"I don't know. I think maybe it was that flyer Charley showed me. And he's got his mind on collectin' that reward for Zane, 'stead of on business."

"Aw, you know Charley. He's a good man. He's just got him a wild hair up his ass over that kid."

"Zane ain't no kid. He's all haired over and full growed. That peckerhead's got more notches on his gun than you got silver dollars in your pocket, Earl. I don't like him bein' here in Santa Fe."

"Who? Charley?" Danvers said.

"No, Zane," Smith said.

He paced the floor while the other two took out storeboughts and lit up. Finally, Smith stopped pacing.

"Shit," he said, "I got to get out of here. We'll wait for the boys downstairs. They're probably tryin' to drink all the tequila down at that cantina."

Earl Crisp didn't say anything. Wayne was such a stickler about secrecy that he kept everybody scattered out, never trusting them all to be together unless they were on a raid or a job. He could have had Charley and the others just come to the Posado instead of having to send Moon to get them and bring them. Grimes, Baker, and Riley still didn't know where Wayne was staying, and wouldn't until they showed up with Moon leading the way.

Danvers got up and walked to the door.

"Put that smoke out, Reed," Smith said. "You'll catch something on fire if you walk down to the lobby with that quirley stuck in your jaw."

"Yes, sir," Danvers said, and craned his neck looking for an ashtray.

"Come on," Wayne said. "Earl, you lead the way. We'll just wait downstairs for the boys."

"Boy, Wayne, you are fidgety tonight," Earl said.

"Yeah, and when I'm fidgety, that means there's a fly in the damned buttermilk. Somethin' ain't right. It's that lawman's instinct, I reckon. Like when everything's going right, that means something's sure as hell going to go wrong."

"Yeah," Earl said. "I know what you mean."

"I don't," Reed said, as he stubbed out his cigarette.

Crisp spit on his cigarette and put the stub in his pocket.

Then the three of them started walking down the stairs to the lobby. That's when they first heard the firecracker popping of gunshots.

"Some kind of Mexican celebration," Crisp said.

"Sounds like gunfire to me," Smith said.

When they got downstairs, the lobby was deserted. The clerk was cowering behind the desk.

"What's going on out there?" Smith asked.

"Mister, there's a hell of a gunfight going on. One of the men who works here went outside with a scattergun and they done blasted him down. He's a-lyin' out there, deader'n a doornail."

"Who the hell's doing the shooting?" Smith asked.

The clerk shrugged. "I don't know," he said, "but they been goin' at it for four or five minutes. Maybe longer."

"Earl, you take a look out there, see what you can see," Smith said to Crisp.

"I hope it ain't our boys," Danvers said.

"Shut up, Reed," Smith said.

"Do I have to?" Earl said.

"Yeah, Earl. Now get to it."

Reluctantly, Earl approached the entrance. They all heard the gunfire, so close sometimes it seemed like it was inside the hotel.

Smith watched Crisp go outside. Saw him stand there a minute, then come running back inside, his face turning a rosy pink from the exertion.

"Well," Smith said. "You see anything?"

"Wayne, I liked to choke on what I saw. I don't know how many are out there, but I saw Charley lyin' there, not movin', and I seen Riley tryin' to hide hisself. Didn't see Kip, but someone's hidin' in the bushes shootin' at someone way down in them trees at the side of the hotel. That ain't all I seen, neither."

"Well, spit it out, Earl," Smith said. "You think we got all night to chew the fat?"

"You know that kid, the one Charley was sayin' was here? Has a thousand-dollar price on his head?"

"Zane?"

"Yeah, that one. He's got him a beard, but it's him all right. He's hiding behind that little wall out there, squarin' off with Riley. He seen me, too, and I skedaddled before he threw down on me."

"You dumb son of a bitch," Smith snarled. "You should have shot him on the spot."

"You just told me to look, Wayne. That's what I did."

Wayne scratched his jaw, let out a sighing breath.

"Well, them boys got themselves into it. It's up to them to get theirselves out," he said. "Let's light a shuck before Zane and whoever else is out there comes in here. I 'spect this place will be swimmin' with lawmen pretty damned quick."

The three men threw their keys on the counter and headed for the rear entrance.

"Do you want a copy of your bill?" the clerk called out. "Are you gents checking out?"

Smith didn't answer.

In moments, the three men were gone, riding their horses into the dark of night. The sound of gunfire faded as they increased the distance between them and the Posado del Rio.

"Where we goin', Wayne?" Crisp asked.

"Someplace where nobody can find us," Smith said, his jaw hardening to stone.

That Lew Wetzel Zane was a thorn in his side, all right.

Maybe he should have gone out there and put his lamp out. He was thinking that, but he had thought the same thing back in Pueblo after he killed Carol and the kids. He had a chance then to kill Zane and, instead, he had hightailed it. Maybe the other man out front was that U.S. marshal he had knocked cold that day in Pueblo. Likely, he thought.

Well, that was two on his list.

Yes, sir, the very next time he saw either one of them, he'd give them lead poisoning.

The bastards.

26

LEW CRAWLED UNDERNEATH THE HORSE. HE FELT ITS CHEST, cradled each ankle with a caressing touch, opened its mouth, and looked at its teeth. This was the horse Marylynn had liked out of all they had seen in the yards, a small steeldust gray with black topknot, mane, and tail. The horse stood about fourteen hands high, he figured. No scars on its hide, no blanket burns.

"Well?" she said when he had finished and stood up. They both stood there, appraising and admiring the horse. The horse eyed them, too, and Lew saw a native intelligence there that raised its value several points.

"A good, sound horse. Gelding, about four years old, good teeth, sound legs."

"Oh, I think he's a beauty, Lew."

"He looks like a big mouse."

"Don't you talk about my horse that way," she said.

"He's not your horse yet. Have to wait until they run him into the arena where you can bid on him."

"How much do you think he will cost?"

"Shouldn't be much. Have to see what the bidding starts at. You could pick him up real cheap."

"When am I going to meet this U.S. marshal? Black-hawk, is that his name?"

"Oh, he'll show up directly. Before noon, I reckon. He's working this morning."

"He almost sounds like a friend, the way he stuck up for you last night at that hotel."

"You mean keeping the local constabulary from dragging me off to jail."

"Yes, and making you a deputy and all."

"A temporary deputy. It suits his purposes. He's not a real friend. If he had Wayne Smith locked up, he'd be dragging me back to Arkansas to stand trial."

"Oh, Lew, I hope he's got more compassion and sense than to do that."

"Oh, he has some compassion, all right. And he's got sense. But he's sworn to uphold the law, and the law says I have to stand trial."

He didn't like to think about it. He knew he would not get a fair trial back in Berryville. He would go up against a hanging judge, and the judge would see to it that he got his neck stretched on the gallows.

The horse walked away. There was the heady scent of sweat, manure, hay, and grain in the air. He had never seen so many horses penned up in one place. There must have been forty head at least in the various corrals. Some looked like Thoroughbreds, and he saw a couple of Spanish Arabians—sleek, black, handsome animals—along with a swaybacked mare or two, several cow ponies with cropped manes and bobbed tails, and even some mules and burros.

They could hear the voice of the auctioneer inside the sales barn, his rapid staccato delivery sounding like a foreign language.

"We'd best get inside, Marylynn," he said. "You don't want to miss bidding on the big mouse."

"Oh, you," she said.

She was wearing her new skirt and boots and the flat-crowned hat that gave her a jaunty look. Lew thought she was a very striking woman and could not help but notice the barely concealed glances other men gave her when she walked by. This morning she looked positively regal and self-assured, which he thought added to her comeliness.

They sat in the middle of the center tier of stadium seats looking down at the horses in the arena, each held by a handler, each haltered. One of the horses drenched the already soggy ground with a stream of yellow urine while another hoisted its tail and left a pile of horse apples that steamed like something recently removed from an oven. The musty scene of the vapors wafted their way while the auctioneer rattled on with his "biddy biddy twenty dollars do I hear twenty-five?"

Finally, a handler led in the steeldust gray gelding. Marylynn perked up. She carried a Mexican fan that she now folded and held in her lap. Her eyes glittered with anticipation.

"Don't look too eager, Marylynn," Lew said. "Let's listen to how the bidding goes."

"Oh, I want to get right in there," she said.

"Wait."

The auctioneer handed some papers to the man next to him, standing just below the pulpit. Then he glanced at another sheet the man handed him.

"This little gelding is four years old, saddle broke, good bottom, good legs, make a fine little cow pony. The bidding will start at ten dollars."

Then he put the paper down and looked up, glancing around the arena at the spectators. Shills stood at various places, acting as spotters for the auctioneer, who would recognize any bidder and acknowledge the bids.

"Well, biddy biddy, I got ten, do I hear twenty, what'llya bid, who'll bid it, ten, I got twelve, lookin' at a bid fifteen, what'llya bid and fifteen, bid it up, bid it up," all in rapid-fire delivery.

"Hold up two fingers," Lew said.

Marylynn held her arm up, two fingers extended.

"Does that mean two dollars more or twenty?" she whispered to Lew.

"Bidup, biddybiddybidup, I got twenty, here's a twenty,

do I hear twenty-five, will he do it, bid it, bid it, bid it, thirty, I got twenty, biddin' it, biddin' it, will it, will it, will it bid up bid up bid uppy twentyfive gimme thirty, gotta get thirty, biddin' it, bid'll it go, what'll it go in a bidup, biddy up, bid gimme thirty . . ."

Marylynn bought the horse for forty dollars. The man she was bidding against dropped out at thirty-eight dollars.

"Good price?" she asked Lew.

"A bargain. You sold that outlaw horse for thirty, so yours cost you only ten bucks."

"That's right," she said, a smile as big as the sunshine on her face.

Lew helped her saddle her new horse, while Marylynn strutted and gloated, petted and raved about it.

"What're you going to name it?" he asked. "Horse needs a name."

"What do you think?" she said.

"Mouse."

"No, no, not Mouse, you cad," she screeched. "He's a noble steed, a wonderful horse. I love him, I just love him. I'll think of a name. Just let me think."

They were getting ready to ride out when Horatio rode up.

"This must be Miss Marylynn Baxter," Blackhawk said, doffing his hat to her.

"Marylynn, this is Marshal Horatio Blackhawk. Horatio, this is Marylynn."

"Let's have some lunch," Blackhawk said. "Follow me. Mighty fine horse you bought, Miss Baxter, a lot of fire in him. He looks like he got all smoked up in one."

"That's it," she exclaimed. "That's what I'm going to name him."

"Fire?" Lew asked, pretending total innocence and ignorance.

"No, no," she protested. "Smoky. That's perfect for him. Look, he loves it."

Smoky was switching his tail up and down, probably swatting at flies, but he did seem to step out when she spoke his name.

Lew smiled.

"Good name," he said.

"Perfect," Blackhawk said.

The marshal led them to a short, squalid street some distance from the main square of Santa Fe. It was called Mercadito, and the street was lined with a number of businesses all selling fresh vegetables, meats, and sundries, mainly to the Mexican population. People strolled, mingled, shopped, sat on wooden crates, smoked, told stories, and hawked their wares, including sandals and clothing. The little cantina/café was called La Boca, and there were tables and chairs both inside and outside. The outside tables sported large umbrellas, which provided shade. A cool breeze blew down the narrow street, and the small roofs in front of the shops provided extra shade.

"Good food here," Blackhawk said while they were tying their horses to a hitching post with several large dowels driven into the wood. He swatted half a dozen flies as he walked Lew and Marylynn inside to a table at the back. He sat at the chair that gave him a good view of he entrance. He indicated that Lew and Marylynn should sit on either side of him.

"You expect trouble here?" Lew said.

Blackhawk shook his head. "Nope. But I like to increase my odds whenever I can."

"Are you a gambling man, Marshal?" Marylynn said.

"No. That's the point. But odds are odds, in life as in cards. And you can call me Blackhawk, if you would."

"Not Blackie," she said, a teasing tone to her voice.

"Not Blackie, thank you."

They all laughed. A young waitress came over and dropped printed cards in front of each of them. The cards were obviously handmade out of heavy cardboard, tinted with some kind of pastel ink or paint. The items on the menu were written in flowing, legible script.

"How did you find this place, Blackhawk?" Lew asked.

"A Santa Fe constable told me about it. They protect the people who work here and keep the criminals out. I thought it would be ideal for our private talk. Also, it's near a place I want to show you. A place where I think, in two days, I'll be able to catch Wayne Smith and arrest him for murder and grand larceny."

They each ordered the luncheon platter: *carne adobo, frijoles, arroz, cebullas, y manzanas fritas.*

"I'm buying," Blackhawk said. "Rather, the United States government is paying."

"Bebidas?" the waitress asked. *"Cerveza, tepache, leche o te."*

They each ordered tea with a slice of lemon.

"Find out anything?" Lew asked after the waitress had left. "What's this about arresting Wayne Smith in a couple of days? That Cinco de Mayo thing?"

"Do you see that poster on the side wall there?" Blackhawk said, inclining his head toward the wall to his left.

"I see it," Marylynn said. "It's in Spanish, though."

Lew read it. It announced a grand celebration of Cinco de Mayo on May 5. This was Tuesday, the third, so the fifth was on Thursday, two days hence.

"What is it?" Lew asked.

"Gringos think it's Mexican Independence Day, but it's not. It marks the day the Mexicans beat the French down in Vera Cruz, driving out Maximilian and his wife, Carlota. Our General Pershing helped the Mexicans beat the French by giving them arms, and the Mexicans have been grateful ever since."

"What has Cinco de Mayo got to do with Wayne Smith?" Lew crunched on a tortilla chip that the waitress had brought in a wicker basket with a napkin lining. He dipped the chip in *salsa casera*, which lit a fire in his mouth.

"The big honcho here in Santa Fe, the head hidalgo, is a man named Hector Lopez de Vega. He's a close friend of Porfirio Diaz, who is the president of Mexico. Every year, on the fifth of May, Lopez sends a stagecoach down to Mexico City as a gift to Porfirio. So it's a celebration of a great victory, and a chance for Santa Fe to show it still cares about their people in Mexico."

"So, just a stagecoach?" Marylynn asked.

Blackhawk smiled. "A stagecoach loaded with money, Marylynn," he said. "With an armed escort, *charros*, who are superb horsemen and crack shots. But I think Smith got to one of Lopez's men, bribed him, and plans to rob that stagecoach before it ever leaves Santa Fe."

"What proof do you have of that?" Lew asked.

"I tracked Moon's movements for the past two months. He bought a lot of drinks for a man named Ernesto Garcia, who works for Lopez. Who is, in fact, like his exchequer, kind of an accountant. Lopez owns a lot of businesses here in Santa Fe and in Taos. He is a very wealthy man. But he's also very tight with his money. Of course, there are resentments among some of his employees. And they resent him sending all that money to Mexico City every year."

"How much money?" Marylynn asked.

"Forty thousand dollars in silver and gold coin," Blackhawk said.

Lew let out a low whistle and reared back in his chair.

A waiter came out with a tray, set their warm plates in front of them. He asked if there was anything else they needed, and Blackhawk told him no and dismissed him.

"So, how do you plan to catch Smith?" Lew asked.

Blackhawk spread a napkin in his lap and picked up a fork.

Marylynn seemed hypnotized. She just sat there and stared at Blackhawk, her eyes wide, glistening like sapphire marbles in the pale light.

Lew swatted at a fly that buzzed in front of his nose and listened to the Mexicans outside chatter in liquid Spanish about the weather and fornication. Laughter bubbled up from the conversations and floated inside the café above the hum of diners speaking in low tones over their meals.

"That's where you come in, Zane," Blackhawk said.

"Me?" Lew said.

"Yeah, you're going to earn your deputy's pay on Thursday, and I'm hoping Miss Marylynn will help you pull it off."

Blackhawk smiled, but said no more as he speared a chunk of *adobo* on his fork, chewing it methodically while trying to suppress a conspiratorial grin.

Lew shook his head. He was beginning to feel a deep sense of dread.

He had no idea what Blackhawk had in mind, but he knew, without asking, that he was liable to end up a dead deputy.

Marylynn started eating and looked at Lew, nodded at him to tend to his meal.

He managed a weak smile, but his stomach churned like a maelstrom of bitter, noxious bile. He wanted to run and take Marylynn with him, run to some place where Blackhawk would never find him, never want to find him.

Someplace far far away.

27

LEW HAD THE EERIE FEELING THAT BLACKHAWK WAS LEADING them through a ghost town. They rode down a deserted street, the vacant windows dark and ominous. Tumbleweeds clung to the rotting boardwalk along a row of crumbling adobes, the lettering on their exteriors long since faded to illegible scrawls. There wasn't a dog or a cat to be seen.

Blackhawk seemed to be enjoying their discomfort. Marylynn looked apprehensive whenever he glanced over at her. She looked so small and vulnerable atop Smoky, but she clutched her handbag with her new pistol in it, as if she were ready to fight at the drop of a Stetson.

They turned onto another street, or what was left of it. The buildings there were all caved in, and debris littered the street—crumpled up old newspapers, part of a small keg, a wagon tongue, a yoke weathered to a gray hulk so that it looked like a cracked bone from some prehistoric beast, rusted tin cans, pieces of leather gnawed by rats, dusty bottles, broken glass, a child's doll, no more than rags with its shredded cloth and eyeless head.

"A small tornado came through here many years ago," Blackhawk said. "Killed people, destroyed everything inside the buildings, scared the hell out of the people. The Mexicans say this place is cursed."

"Horatio, you're scaring me," Marylynn said.

"Don't mean to. Just a little bit of history in case you were wondering."

"I'm wondering why in hell you brought us here," Lew said. His stomach had started to roil again, and he could hear the wind keening through the open windows, whispering in the shadows of old broken adobes. "It's like a ghost town."

"That's just what it is, really," Blackhawk said. "And I think that's why Lopez de Vega chose it for his annual mission."

Then, all of a sudden, there it was. They came upon an old abandoned freight office, with a loading ramp of broken and weathered boards and a faded sign that read RENALDO FREIGHT & HAULING. Two old corrals attested to its abandonment, with only a few gray poles standing, others stacked up in a pile of tumbleweeds and blown sand.

A jackrabbit stared at them, then bolted away, bounding over detritus that was unidentifiable.

"There it is," Blackhawk said. "Renaldo was killed when the twister roared through here."

On the other side, they saw the ruins of wagons, with spokeless wheels twisted into shapes that bore no geometric identities, and there were the bones of horses, stark and white as if they had been bleached, and skulls, their empty sockets seeming to stare at them from a nameless graveyard.

"This place gives me the shivers," Marylynn said.

Lew nodded. Even in the glare of the hot sun, he could feel a chill.

"This is where it will all happen on Thursday," Blackhawk said. "That morning, the Concord will pull up and the escort assemble. Two men will arrive in a wagon with a strongbox filled with gold and silver coins in the amount of five thousand dollars. These are symbolic, only. The remaining thirty-five thousand dollars will be in bank notes, negotiable anywhere. The box will be locked with a heavy padlock. There will be a brief ceremony as the money is transferred to the stagecoach. Lopez de Vega will give a speech. A small band will play the Mexican national anthem and the song they play at bullfights, something to do with 'no quarter.' Then, the coach will leave, with the *charros* carrying rifles, wearing their bright costumes. People will cheer, and this place will go quiet again when everybody leaves."

"And this is where Wayne Smith is going to make his move?" Lew said.

"He purchased dynamite two days ago, ten sticks of DuPont 60/40, and blasting caps. He'll kill a lot of people to get that money."

"The police will stop him?" Lew said.

"Follow me. I'll lay the whole scheme out for you, Lew."

They rode back to the deserted street. The wind blew a tumbleweed down its center and whined in the empty adobes.

"There will be constabulary in some of the buildings. I'll be on the roof of that adobe, with my rifle. Smith and his men will ride through here to the freight yard."

"And you'll shoot him?" Marylynn said.

"It won't be that simple," Blackhawk said.

"Nothing ever is," Lew said.

"We think Smith will have innocent people with him. And when he comes through here, the fuses will be lit on those sticks of dynamite."

"Can't you find out who he's bringing with him and warn them not to come?" Lew asked.

"That part of it is unknown to me and the police here. But he pulled the same stunt in Denver when he robbed Horace Tabor."

"What did he do?" Marylynn asked.

"He invited a number of important dignitaries to come and tour the Tabor Opera House. They were in the way, and innocent, so Smith got away while the dignitaries got in the way of any pursuit."

"Pretty smart," Lew said.

"Oh, he's smart all right. I just don't know what he has planned for this robbery. But he won't be alone."

"So how will you get him?" Lew asked.

"That's where you come in, Lew. You and Marylynn, if she'll do it.

"I don't like the sound of this, Horatio."

"Don't worry. You'll be covered. See that first adobe there? Not much left of it, but enough to keep you hidden until the right time."

"What's the right time?" Lew asked.

"I'm betting that Smith will want you dead as bad as he wants the money. Those fuses are timed. He'll likely light them as soon as he passes that first building. We've got to stop him before he gets that far. If there are no people in the way, no innocents, we can shoot. We have to separate him from those people."

"And I'm the bait," Lew said.

"Yep. 'Fraid so. When I see Smith coming, I'll give you a signal from that roof over there. You'll be able to see me, but Smith won't see you. Until you step out. Marylynn will let out a scream from her hiding place just as you do. That'll get Smith's attention. When he sees you, he'll try and drop you. But you'll duck back in real quick, so that he has to come after you. Marylynn will scream again after you've taken cover. He'll have to shut her up."

"Sounds way too complicated," Lew said.

"It'll work, because I know how Wayne Smith thinks. He's greedy, but you are a witness to murder, and you had something to do with his wife. He's got a temper raw as a boil. He'll come after you. That's when we'll get him."

Lew dismounted and walked into the ruined adobe, while Blackhawk and Marylynn looked on. He emerged a few minutes later.

"Pretty skimpy," Lew said.

"Enough," Blackhawk said. He looked at Marylynn. "How about you? You game to play a part in this, young lady?"

"I wouldn't miss it for the world," she said.

Lew stared at her as if she were addled.

It could work, he thought. Blackhawk seemed to have thought it all out pretty carefully. But in such a situation, a lot could go wrong, and probably would.

Still, if that was the way to stop Wayne Smith and either kill him or arrest him, he had to try.

He nodded to Blackhawk.

"I'll do it," he said.

"I knew you would, Lew," he said.

In the distance a quail called, its fluting cry sounding solemn in the stillness, as if it were warning its brethren to beware. Death was there in that lonesome place, and the wind carried the memory of what had happened there years before, and perhaps knew what was going to happen there on Cinco de Mayo.

Lew shivered in the afternoon sun.

28

LEW BRUSHED THE SLENDER STRANDS OF SILK FROM HIS FACE. Cobwebs clung to his trousers, mingled with the dust on his boots, while spiders crawled along the wind-blasted wall of the damaged adobe. Dust filled his nostrils, danced in the rays of sunlight streaming into the dilapidated adobe while he stood in concealment, waiting. In the corner next to him, Marylynn sat on adobe bricks she had stacked there for that purpose.

"One thing, Marylynn," he said. "When you go to screaming, like Horatio asked, don't just scream. Call out Wayne's name. That'll surely get his attention."

"You want me to yell out 'Wayne'?"

"Yes. He might think it's the ghost of his murdered wife."

From his position in back of a window, Lew could see Blackhawk atop a two-story building just across the street. Rather, he could see the crown of his hat and the tip of his rifle barrel. Policemen were stationed in the other adobes along the street, men who had been there since shortly after dawn.

Blackhawk had said the ceremonies would start early, around eight o'clock, since the stage driver wanted to leave while it was still relatively cool.

"The wagon with the strongbox should be here about fifteen minutes later," he said, "and Smith will come along pretty quick after that."

"You sound pretty sure of yourself, Horatio."

"I know what makes Smith's pony gallop," he said.

They heard the band tune up, and a few minutes later, they began to play "La Macarena."

"Must be getting close," Lew said.

"My stomach's full of butterflies," Marylynn said.

"Just remember to stay where you are when the shooting starts."

"I will. But I'm keeping my pistol right here in my lap. Just in case that mean old Wayne comes busting in here."

"He won't get this far. Either Horatio will shoot him, or I will."

A wagon rumbled down the street. Lew watched it pass by. Two men sat on the buckboard seat, a third, with a rifle, was in the back, facing the rear. The top of the strongbox was just barely visible. Lew felt his stomach roil. He hadn't eaten breakfast. He had drunk some coffee, just enough to pry open all his senses and tune them up, like the men had done with their guitars, the trumpet, and the tambour.

The wagon stopped, and so did the band. Lew heard someone call the spectators over to hear the speech by Lopez de Vega. As soon as he began speaking, Lew saw Blackhawk give the signal that Smith was approaching. He looked over at Marylynn, who still sat on the stacked adobe bricks, holding her pistol in her lap.

"Here he comes," he whispered.

Marylynn sat up straight and held the Smith & Wesson ready.

Lew listened, his ear close to the window.

What he heard made his heart pound faster, sweat break out on his forehead.

Children.

He heard children laughing and talking as they marched toward him. He walked away from the window and stood next to the door. He put his face close to the jamb and edged it outward so that he could just barely see the odd assemblage walking toward him. No, they were not walking. They were jumping up and down, skipping, jogging back and forth in their ranks. Three nuns, wearing severe habits and gull wing headgear, flanked the children. Their rosary beads glistened in the sun and silver glinted off their crucifixes.

Lew's heart plummeted in his chest when he saw the sisters from Our Lady of Guadalupe Orphanage. They looked like angels.

Angels of death in their black habits.

He looked up at Blackhawk.

No sign of him.

Lew got ready. As soon as the first children passed the window, he looked out again. Behind the children, he saw Wayne Smith and two other men. Two of the men were holding sticks of dynamite in their hands. Wayne was riding just behind them, a rifle lying across the pommel. His hands held on to it, and his fingers were inside the trigger guard.

"Now," Lew whispered to Marylynn and stepped out into the street.

"Hey, Wayne, you son of a bitch," Lew yelled. The two men stopped their horses.

Lew drew his pistol.

Wayne started to bring his rifle up.

Marylynn screamed at the top of her lungs, "Waaaaaayyyyyyyne."

The effect of her voice on Lew was bone-chilling.

Wayne looked startled.

The two men in front reacted. They stuffed dynamite in the pockets of their dusters, leaving one hand free. Both drew their pistols. Wayne brought up the rifle.

Then Lew ducked back inside the adobe.

"Again," he told Marylynn.

Marylynn screamed again, "Waaaaaaayyyyyyynnnne."

Wayne turned his horse toward the adobe and put the spurs to its flanks.

The two men in front started firing their pistols.

Bullets smacked into the adobe. One came whooshing through the window and struck an old rusted can in the back corner.

"I'll get him," Wayne shouted to his men, Crisp and Danvers. "Don't shoot no more."

The children started screaming. They scattered like chickens when Smith galloped past, their high-pitched voices turning shrill as they fled.

"Light 'em," Wayne yelled as he charged toward the adobe where Lew and Marylynn were hiding.

Blackhawk stood up and leveled his rifle at Smith.

Smith leaned over to the side of his horse and snatched up a little girl who was frozen to the ground and screaming in terror. He plunked her on his lap, and Blackhawk lowered his rifle.

"Lew, look out," Blackhawk called.

Crisp struck a match and lit a fuse on one of the sticks of dynamite. Sparks made a small orange fountain.

Danvers fumbled for a match.

"Up on the roof, Earl," Danvers yelled. He reined his horse in a tight turn.

Crisp twisted in his saddle and saw Blackhawk. He drew back his arm to throw the stick of dynamite straight at him. As he started to throw, Blackhawk squeezed the trigger.

The rifle barked, spat flame and smoke.

Crisp never completed the toss.

The bullet sliced through the top of his left shoulder, burning a furrow in his flesh. He didn't cry out, just winced with the sharp pain. But he had to draw his arm back for another try at throwing the stick of dynamite.

Blackhawk levered another cartridge into the chamber. The empty hull flew out and clattered atop the building.

Reed Danvers thumbed back the hammer on his six-gun and fired off a shot at Blackhawk. But his horse was moving and his aim was off. The bullet missed Blackhawk by a foot. He heard the air swish in his ear as the bullet passed while he was drawing another bead on Crisp.

Marylynn stood up and went to the window to see what was going on. People down the street were screaming now, adding to the noise the children were making.

Lew stepped to the doorway as Smith, holding the little girl, reined to a halt a few feet from the adobe. He shoved the barrel of his pistol against the girl's temple.

"Step out, Zane, or I'll blow this little girl's head clean off."

Marylynn gasped when she saw what was happening.

"Lew," she rasped, "do something or he'll murder that child."

A thousand thoughts rambled through Lew's brain. They tripped over one another, got tangled up, floundered. A lifetime seemed to pass in the space of a split second. He saw the girl's terrified face, the tears leaving tracks on her cheeks, her eyes wide with fear.

And he saw the slitted eyes of Wayne Smith, the taut expression of hatred on his face, the cocked hammer of his single action Colt, his finger curling around the trigger.

Another lifetime passed in the space of a half second. The screams and the cries of the people down the street seemed to fade as if he had cotton in his ears. His pistol was cocked, his finger on the trigger.

Time stopped dead in its tracks.

Blackhawk fired his rifle again just as Crisp started to hurl the stick of dynamite with its hissing fuse.

The bullet from his Winchester hit Crisp square in the breastbone with the force of a flung hammer multiplied a hundred times. There was the crack of bone, and blood spurted from Crisp's chest like wine gushing through a bunghole in a cask. Blood bubbled up in Crisp's throat, strangling him, drowning him. The dynamite smacked against the wall of the adobe just below where Blackhawk stood on its roof. A nun and three children saw the sputtering fuse and eyed it as they would a wriggling snake, frozen in fear. Then the nun recovered her senses and started herding the children away from the dynamite. She looked like a giant bird with her chicks.

Danvers raised his pistol, took dead aim on Blackhawk.

A thousand lifetimes collapsed in a heap, occupying the space of a single second in time.

Lew had no target. The girl in Smith's lap completely blocked Smith's body. Only his face showed, next to the pistol in his hand, a face that mirrored the hatred inside the man. The girl no longer struggled. She just stared down at

Lew with terror crawling across her face, lighting her wide
eyes with the gleam of imminent death.

"I said drop it, Zane," Smith said. "Or this girl is wolf
meat in two seconds."

It was then that Lew made his decision. He could die
there without a fight. He knew if he dropped his gun, Smith
would turn his pistol on him and shoot him dead where he
stood.

Or he could shoot through the girl and hope to hit Smith
in the heart, killing them both.

He had just one chance to save the girl and himself.

Smith's face loomed large in Lew's eyes. It was a target.
He was no more than ten feet away.

Was he that good a shot?

There was no time to reason it out. Two seconds wasn't
very long for a man to make up his mind.

The wind came up, that same deathwind that always
seemed to arrive when Lew was in a fight and about to kill
or be killed. It blew down the street and made dust swirl in
spidery gyrations all along its path.

Lew summoned up all of his courage and confidence and
extended his arm. The action was so fast, his motion was
only a blur. And he sighted across the blade sight and saw
that face of Smith's, bigger than an elephant. He held his
breath and squeezed the trigger.

There wasn't even a look of surprise on Smith's face
when the bullet smashed through his forehead and blew his
brains to a pulpy mush. The back of his skull blew off and
sailed through the air like a small pie plate. Blood spurted all
over the little girl's hair.

Smith's arm went limp and the girl slid from the saddle,
squirming out of his grasp. She hit the ground and crumpled
up, folding her arms over her head for protection.

The pistol slipped from Smith's grasp. His eyes glazed
over in the frost of death and turned dull in the sunlight before he tumbled over and fell to the ground on the other side.

Danvers heard the shot and turned around.

Lew didn't even hesitate.

He shot Danvers out of the saddle, his bullet striking him

high in the chest, just below his throat. Danvers fell to the ground in a heap.

The dynamite stick exploded.

A cloud of smoke billowed into the adobe and out into the street and up in the air. Adobe sand flew in all directions, filled the street with a brown haze.

Blackhawk felt the building shake, and spread his legs to keep from falling down.

Marylynn screamed.

A thousand lifetimes faded into memory.

The wind died suddenly.

There was a silence as the dust settled to the ground like brown snow, so fine it disappeared, became part of the earth once again.

"Blackhawk didn't even get a chance to thank you for your help," Marylynn said to Lew as they were riding away from Santa Fe, heading south into the blazing afternoon. "I didn't even have a chance to see about all those children." '

"Horatio would have arrested me," Lew said. "He was duty bound."

"Are you always going to be a fugitive from the law, Lew?"

"I don't know," he said. "We'll see how we do in Socorro."

"Isn't there trouble down there?" she asked. "I heard Mr. Blackhawk say something about a marshal going there."

"There's trouble everywhere, Marylynn. I told you not to come with me."

"Where you go, I go," she said.

The sun played tricks on Lew's eyes. He saw a shining lake in the distance, its waters shimmering in the sunlight like fountains of pure silver. It was a beautiful sight to see, and like all good or worthwhile things in life, it would vanish as soon as he got close enough to stop and drink his fill.

GROSS
and Disgusting
THINGS
About the Human Body

by Joanna Emery
with illustrations by Roger Garcia

BLUE
BIKE
BOOKS

The Publisher: Blue Bike Books
www.bluebikebooks.com

Library and Archives Canada Cataloguing in Publication

Emery, Joanna, 1966–
Gross and disgusting things about the human body / Joanna Emery.

ISBN-13: 978-1-897278-25-3
ISBN-10: 1-897278-25-X

  1. Body, Human—Humor. 2. Body, Human—Miscellanea. I. Title.

QP38.E45 2007   612   C2007-901526-3

Project Director: Nicholle Carrière
Project Editor: Kathy van Denderen
Cover Designer: Jay Dirto
Book Designer: Anne Iles
Illustrations: Roger Garcia

Photography Credits: Every effort has been made to accurately
credit the sources of photographs. Any errors or omissions should be
directed to the publisher for changes in future editions. Photographs
courtesy of CDC/Dr. Heinz F. Eichenwald, 1958 (p.76); Julie
Dermansky (p.23); Dreamstime (p.16, Stephen Sweet/1766010; p.81,
Pirus01/408673; p.89, Jenny Horne/1193410; p.98, Teoteoteo/1461963;
p.101, Suzanne Tucker/1624633); http://www.ooze.com/ooze13/
petomane.html (p.147); MissingLink, UCSF Instructional Grant
Program, the Center for Instructional Technology, and the School of
Medicine Dean's Office, University of California Regents (p.187); NCI
Visuals Online from the collections of the Office of Communications,
National Cancer Institute (p.26, Dr. Leon Kaufman/AV-8900-4145);
Wikibooks (p.227).

PC: P5